"I need a wife, *elika*," Stelios murmured.

Petra shuddered as he went on, "A marriage in exchange for sons is what I offer. A marriage that calls for little sacrifice for a girl badly in need of a protector...."

She was too shocked to speak. Finally she managed, "You expect me to marry you because you lied to the police and told them Gavin was your future brother-in-law? I love him dearly, but that won't allow me to be drawn into such a disastrous agreement!"

Stelios recoiled sharply, as though shocked by her ingratitude.

"Then you leave me little choice. I shall inform the police that our wedding is canceled and your brother is no longer in my custody. They will deal with him as they see fit."

Books by Margaret Rome

These books may be available at your local bookseller.

For a free catalog listing all titles currently available,
send your name and address to:

Harlequin Reader Service
P.O. Box 52040, Phoenix, AZ 85072-2040
Canadian address: Stratford, Ontario N5A 6W2

Castle of the Lion

Margaret Rome

Harlequin Books

TORONTO • NEW YORK • LONDON
AMSTERDAM • PARIS • SYDNEY • HAMBURG
STOCKHOLM • ATHENS • TOKYO • MILAN

Original hardcover edition published in 1983
by Mills & Boon Limited

ISBN 0-373-02615-3

Harlequin Romance first edition April 1984

CHAPTER ONE

PETRA heard the telephone ringing the moment she arrived outside the door of her flat. Hastily she dumped her briefcase, shopping bag and umbrella on the ground and began rummaging through her handbag for the key which, whenever it was needed in a hurry, seemed to adopt an annoying habit of playing hide and seek among folds of silken lining. An age seemed to elapse before her groping fingers pounced upon their prey, frantic, frowning seconds during which her mind offered, then rejected, various suggestions as to the possible identity of the caller. It could not be her brother Gavin, for less than eight hours previously she had driven him to the airport, then had waited until, with considerable relief, she had seen him board a 'plane bound for Cyprus and their grandfather's home where he had arranged to spend his vacation.

Nor was the caller, whose prolonged summons seemed to be growing louder with each passing second, likely to be her boss. Imperious, demanding, exacting though he undoubtedly was, Sir Joseph Holland had promised her a full weekend off and, as befitted one of Britain's premier diplomats, he had proved himself often, during their long and happy association, to be a man of his word.

She turned the key in the latch, scooped her

belongings from the ground to dump them inside the tiny hallway, then kicked shut the door before racing to pluck the telephone receiver from its rest. 'Hello! Petra Morrison speaking, can I help you?' she questioned in a breathless rush.

A premonition of trouble disturbed her senses when a thickly accented voice repeated her name and telephone number before demanding. 'Will you accept a reverse charge call from Larnaca, Cyprus?' *Why a reverse charge call?* she almost startled aloud, before reason took over, reminding her that the operator was merely carrying out normal procedure and was therefore unlikely to be qualified to supply answers to personal questions.

'Yes ... yes, of course,' she stammered, momentarily losing the cool that had earned her a reputation for poised equanimity among her colleagues in the Diplomatic Corps.

'Go ahead, caller!'

The operator's final words were eclipsed by a jerky voice Petra had difficulty identifying as that of her usually happy-go-lucky student brother.

'Petra, where the dickens have you been all afternoon? I've been trying for the past couple of hours to get through to you and I've only just managed to persuade them to allow me one last attempt. They seem to have formed an impression that I'm fooling around—merely playing for time!'

Petra frowned, completely puzzled. 'I worked later than usual at the office to clear my desk of odds and ends,' she explained briefly, 'then went shopping for enough food to last me over the weekend. What's wrong, Gavin, are you in some sort of trouble? And who on earth are *they* . . .?'

'I'm sorry, Sis,' her brother mumbled, sounding completely dispirited, 'I'd like to soften the blow, but as I suspect from the scowls that are being directed my way that I'm likely to be cut off any minute I'd better cut out the frills and come straight to the point. I've been arrested! *They* are the police who detained me when I tried to pass through Customs. They've accused me of attempting to smuggle dope into the country, but I swear to you, Sis, that I have no idea how the reefer cigarette ends got into my anorak pocket! The only feasible explanation I can think of is that some witless baboon decided to play a hideous practical joke on me during last night's end-of-term party. Believe me, I've never touched anything of that nature—nor even felt tempted to do so. But judging from the reaction of the Greek police they apparently suspect me of masterminding some international drug ring at the very least!'

'You're joking, of course!' Even at that moment of stunned incredulity a tiny portion of Petra's clinical mind marvelled at the miracle of trite, feeble words whispered inside a London flat becoming audible to a listener in far-off Cyprus.

Proof that the miracle had actually happened was supplied by Gavin's anguished reply.

'How I wish I were! At first I tried to kid myself that I was experiencing a nightmare that would vanish when I woke up, but these black-browed policemen are real, the bars around my cell are made of steel. I'm in one hell of a fix, Sis! You must do something to get me out of here!'

Though her heart and pulses were threatening hysteria, Petra's ice cool mind began ticking over, telling her that recriminations would be useless at this stage, that Gavin's most urgent need was for action by someone in authority.

'Have you managed to get in touch with Grandfather, he might be able to help?'

She winced away from the phone when Gavin's voice exploded against her eardrum.

'Patera Romios is well known and highly respected in his own small area, but he has no real clout,' he dismissed crudely. 'Besides that,' his voice dropped to a pitch of despondency, 'you know how fanatically he regards family honour—his fierce Greek pride would never allow him to forgive me if ever he were to find out . . .'

When his voice trailed into miserable silence Petra's heart lurched, concern for his safety prompting from her lips the reckless promise.

'Don't worry, Gavin, leave everything to me. Somehow or other I'll find a way to secure your release!' His heartfelt sigh of relief caressed her ear as she rummaged through a drawer in search of a notepad and pencil. 'First of all, I'll need some details—the name of the officer in charge, for instance. I'll write to him. No, on second thoughts, it might be better if I were to take a few days' leave and visit Cyprus to plead your cause in person,' she decided, waiting with pencil poised.

'That would be an utter waste of time and you know it!' With a savage frustration that caused her to hold the earpiece a few inches distant, Gavin reminded her, 'I've lost count of the times I've heard you criticising the chauvinistic attitude of the average Greek male, the patronising manner he adopts towards his womenfolk; his refusal to listen to, much less take seriously, any argument attempted by a female. Even if you were to supply the authorities with proof of your academic brilliance or the status you've achieved in the Foreign Office they would refuse to be impressed! I hate asking you to plead on my behalf, Petra, but as your boss, Sir Joseph Holland, is the only man of our acquaintance possessing power enough to cut any ice with this crowd, I must beg you to approach him for help. *Please, Petra*—I know how you feel about the abuse of authority, your distaste of the notion of using position to extract privileges, but because my situation is so desperate I'm asking you, just this once, to set aside your principles and ask Sir Joseph to intercede on my behalf!'

'*No!*' she gasped with revulsion, but her emphatic refusal coincided with a sharp click as the line when dead. 'Gavin! Gavin, are you still there!' she called out, reluctant to believe that she had been cut off in mid-sentence, leaving her brother pinning his hopes of release upon a false assumption that she would be prepared to sacrifice cherished precepts of honour, fair play, and very probably the respect of a boss whose values ran parallel with her own, in order to extricate him from the consequences of what was probably no more than a student prank gone badly wrong.

Slowly she dropped the receiver on to its cradle, then wandered, still dazed, into the kitchen where mechanically she began storing away the groceries she had bought—packets of biscuits into an airtight tin; bacon, eggs and milk inside the fridge; a few tins of soup, peas, fruit, and a jar of instant coffee on to the shelves of a cupboard that was practically bare. The task acted as an anaesthetic, keeping her mind numb, putting off the moment of idleness that would force her to face facts, to decide upon a choice of direction between two roads—one signposted shame, the other humiliation.

But by the time she had prepared prawns, tossed a salad, and begun laying the table for her evening meal, the initial shock of Gavin's words had subsided and the art of calm, logical reasoning that had played such a major part in her spectacular rise through the ranks of the Diplomatic Corps had taken over control of her emotions.

Gavin, she decided, buttering the crusty rolls she had bought at the bakers, was still an irresponsible boy at heart, prone to wild flights of imagination, spoiled from birth by their doting Greek mother whose death two years ago—and so soon after the accident that had deprived them of their father— had inflicted such pain and grief that instinctively she and Gavin had clung to each other, two distraught orphans, one determined to do everything necessary to protect and comfort her schoolboy brother, the other urgently in need of a surrogate mother.

Unfortunately, Gavin had continued to cling and was clinging still. Even though he had inherited his fair share of their father's mental agility, a strong strain of Greek blood, together with his mother's earlier spoiling, had combined to form a character who accepted cynosure as a right, who demanded of his womenfolk an abundance of love that would admit no flaw.

Petra sighed, lifting a shaking hand to sweep a heavy wing of hair back from her furrowed brow. As it sprang silken beneath her fingers memories swamped her, memories of the father whose Saxon fairness both she and her brother had inherited, but whose placid nature had been passed on to her alone. How often she had crept on to his knee in search of the sort of solace that can only be enjoyed in the company of a kindred spirit! How she had loved to tease him by tweaking his hair before bracing her childish frame for the punishing bearhug that had always preceded his fondly growled threat:

'You must be taught a lesson, Honeybun, so that when you're grown up you'll remember that, however busy a bee might appear, however indifferent, he'll react with a sting to torment!'

Her pensive expression brightened as the pet name used exclusively by him echoed down the years. Then just as suddenly her humorous half-smile faded as she recalled with a wince the mocking title bestowed by office juniors that never failed to hurt. *Miss Grundy!*

What *will* Miss Grundy say? . . . What *will* Miss Grundy think? . . .

Daily, although never intentionally within her hearing, the catch-phrases were tossed around the outer office by typists and clerks no younger than herself, but lacking the qualifications, the status, the responsibility and strain of mothering a younger brother, that made her appear aloof, prim and straightlaced to their insensitive eyes. If only they knew, she reflected sadly, how urgently and often she felt the need to kick over the traces, how she envied them their ability to dance, to date, to feel completely carefree . . .

Mechanically, she slid open a drawer in search of table mats. Immediately Gavin's frantic warning returned to haunt her when her fingers made contact with gay, attractive mats woven in the small mountain village that had been her mother's home, where every woman had a loom in her house and wove all her own furnishing needs as well as yards and yards of material used to supply husbands and sons with *vraka*, the traditional baggy pants favoured by the tough, hardworking men of the mountains.

Forgotten snatches of conversation exchanged between herself and her grandfather which she had found amusing at the time echoed sinisterly, casting doubt upon her ability to argue her brother's cause with men arrogant enough to have become enraged by their government's attempt to change marital laws that rendered wives mere chattels.

'But, Patera,' she had dared to remonstrate, 'your country's present laws are unfair and deeply humiliating to women. Why should Greek wives be debarred from legally càrrying out any financial transaction? Or from spending a night away from home without their husband's permission? As the law now stands, wives are not allowed even to enrol their children in a school, and husbands have the right of access to all their letters! Do you realise, I wonder, that Greece is the only Western country where adultery is still punishable by imprisonment?'

'And so it should remain!' Her grandfather's fist

had thumped down hard upon the arm of his chair. Angrily, moustache bristling with the force of his emotions, he had dismissed her emancipated argument with a gesture of deep contempt. 'What is the world coming to if a man is to be deprived of his right—after finding his wife in bed with another man—to march the two of them, still undressed, to the nearest police station in order to secure his evidence? And as for the suggestion of allowing civil marriages,' he had snorted, 'the Church would refuse to countenance, much less bless, such unholy alliances!'

He had stumped out of his small, sparsely furnished house to rendezvous with elderly cronies who were always to be found in animated conversation seated around a tiny metal table placed outside the taverna in the village square.

Petra pushed in the drawer, deprived of all appetite for food by churning fear—fear for Gavin's safety, fear of men whose national characteristics were intolerance of weakness, specifically masculine weakness, and a dedicated belief that such a crime against their macho image could only be expunged by the sort of toughening-up process which Petra felt certain would be freely available inside primitive Greek jails.

She rushed almost without volition towards the telephone in the hall, fumbled out a number on the dial, then waited tense with anxiety for a response from the other end. Immediately she heard her boss's gruff tone, she blurted:

'Sir Joseph, this is Petra Morrison speaking. I'd like your opinion on a matter of great importance, if you can spare me half an hour of your time?'

'Now, d'you mean?' She could picture piercing grey eyes scanning a watch. 'My dear Petra, your conscientious application to work sets a worthy example to everyone in the department, but as it's almost eight-thirty and my wife is waiting to be taken out to dinner. I do think that whatever problem is on your mind can't become more aggravated by being left until Monday morning!'

'Oh, but it could, and almost certainly will!' she cried out in her alarm, imagining him preparing to lower the receiver. 'And the matter I want to discuss has nothing to do with the department, it's ... it's a personal problem,' she faltered lamely.

The pause that followed seemed indicative of surprise. Sir Joseph was seldom lost for words, but his response, though hesitant, was kind and very firm.

'Then by all means come round to my flat immediately. My wife won't mind a short delay—in fact, I'm certain she will insist upon your joining us for dinner once she's made aware of your visit.'

'Oh, no, I couldn't possibly,' she jerked, then pulled up short, appalled by the ungraciously phrased refusal. 'I'm sorry,' she gulped, unnerved to the point of tears, 'I didn't mean to sound so impolite. It's just that ... I'm far too worried to be able to do justice to a meal.'

'In that case, my dear,' Sir Joseph instructed briskly, 'let's waste no further time talking over the phone. As you're obviously too upset to drive I'll order a taxi. Be prepared for its arrival in about ten minutes' time.'

Less than half an hour later Petra was being

ushered into the flat grown familiar to her during
the many occasions when she had helped Lady
Holland to prepare for and entertain visiting
foreign diplomats at quiet, informal dinner parties.

'Fate appears to be on your side, my dear,' Sir
Joseph smiled as he took her coat. 'My wife and I
usually leave for our country home on Friday
afternoon, but as no guests have been invited to
stay the weekend and my wife had some last-
minute business to attend to, we decided to spend
tonight here at the flat and make our leisurely way
home in the morning.'

'It's very kind of you to allow my problems to
intrude into your privacy, Sir Joseph,' she
mumbled with eyes downcast, feeling suddenly shy
of the boss whose stature had never appeared
more imposing, his eyes more reassuring, his
attitude more kindly disposed.

'Go straight to my study where we can talk
without fear of interruption.' Cupping a hand
beneath her elbow, he ushered her forward,
containing his curiosity until they were both seated
inside a book-lined study crammed with a treasure
trove of souvenirs gleaned during years of world
travel.

'Can I get you a drink—a brandy, perhaps . . .?'
His shrewd eyes questioned her deeper than usual
pallor, the sensitive trembling of a sweetly shaped
mouth that often appeared too stern, too firmly
constricted.

'No, thank you, Sir Joseph.' He was in the act
of turning away from the drinks cabinet, obviously
not inclined to argue with her prim refusal, when
she astonished him with an uncharacteristic show

of indecision. 'Oh, well, perhaps just a small one . . .'

His bushy grey eyebrows rose, but without comment he poured out two measures of cognac, set her glass down upon an occasional table, then returned to his seat with his own glass cupped between his palms.

'Now that the proprieties have been observed,' he teased gently, 'perhaps we can proceed to sort out the problem that has rendered my very capable assistant a fluster of nerves? It must be the very first time in our acquaintance,' he mused, watching silken lashes fluttering nervously as moths against waxen cheeks, 'that you've asked for advice about your personal affairs. I feel pleased and flattered to be the one chosen to render assistance.'

He continued chatting easily, giving the cognac time to work its relaxing magic upon a slim form made tense by the humiliation of being forced to share a family secret.

'My wife and I have often wondered why you've always been so reluctant to accept invitations to join us for a break at our home in the country. Since early youth you appear to have concentrated on your scholastic career with a dedication that shut out all human contact, except, of course for that of your brother. Head girl at school; brilliant student, talented university graduate—the praises of those who have followed your career are endless. Adjectives I've heard used are—highly intelligent, honest, reliable, loyal, nevertheless, it strikes me that a cultured young woman needs more than a good background and education to prepare her for life in the outside world.' He leant forward to stress: '*The real world*, Petra, where there's excitement and glamour to be found, where there are parties and love affairs during which one learns to lean on another's strength and to tolerate another's weaknesses!'

He realised that his lecture had barely impressed itself upon her troubled mind when a heavy fan of lashes lifted over eyes so blue that their impact never failed to leave him startled. 'I wouldn't dream of sacrificing my career for the sake of a good time, Sir Joseph, I have more important matters to deal with during the small amount of leisure time that's available. Anyway,' she dismissed with a shrug, 'the party circuit doesn't appeal to me, neither am I very much inclined towards men, alcohol, or silly social activities.' With a nervous gulp she drained her glass, then as she set it carefully down upon the table he sensed that she was about to bare her soul.

'Sir Joseph . . .'

'Yes, my dear?' he encouraged cautiously.

'You must have heard me speak of my brother Gavin?'

'Yes, of course.' He leant back in his chair and frowned, disappointed by the discovery that his suspicion had been proved correct. Gavin Morrison, whom he had once heard described by a member of his student brotherhood as a retarded adolescent, was following his usual practice of unloading self-inflicted burdens upon his sister's slender shoulders.

'I saw him to the airport this morning where he

caught a plane for Cyprus. Unfortunately,' Petra gulped, 'on his arrival he was arrested!'

'Good lord!' Sir Joseph jerked upright, spilling brandy over immaculately pressed trousers.

'Gavin's done nothing wrong,' she hastened to assure him, 'nothing other than become the victim of a stupid prank that went tragically wrong! He's been accused by the police of attempting to smuggle dope into the country. The Greek authorities have persistently ignored his explanation and have flatly refused to allow him out of gaol.'

'The silly young ass!' Sir Joseph exploded loudly. 'I assume that whatever drugs were found upon his person were a complete mystery to him!'

'Exactly,' she confirmed eagerly, totally oblivious of his sarcasm. 'He thinks the reefer cigarette ends may have been planted in his pocket by a fellow student, but that's merely theory and can't be proved conclusively.'

Her boss snorted, then in a tightly controlled tone he used only when violently aggravated, spelled out plainly:

'I'm sorry, Petra, I'd like to help, if only for your sake, but there's nothing I can do in my professional capacity, because the Greeks, more than any other nationality, have made it quite plain in the past that their resentment of the attempts of foreign diplomats to interfere in matters of internal policy runs deep as the seas around their islands. To be blunt, my dear, the island of Cyprus in particular has often been referred to by my colleagues as a political tightrope. One false step made by myself, or by any member of my department, could place all our careers in jeopardy.'

Petra jumped to her feet. 'You surely can't expect me to do nothing about my brother being falsely arrested and incarcerated inside a Greek gaol!' Her agitation was so great she forgot her shyness, forgot even that the man she was berating was her superior, a man highly rated in diplomatic circles for his shrewdness, integrity, and devotion to duty.

'I most certainly do!' Sir Joseph rose to tower over her. 'The position of authority you hold in the Diplomatic Corps demands that your brother's situation must be allowed to run its natural course. Any action of yours—were it to become known that you're second in command to a senior British diplomat—could be construed as a breach of privilege. Members of our profession must be above reproach, we cannot be as free as others to act in any way we wish, especially abroad,' he reminded sternly. 'On the contrary, we're expected, indeed, it's our bounden duty, to act at all times as ambassadors of our government!'

Petra stared, shaken to the core by the unaccustomed reprimand. But in spite of his stern call to duty, in spite of his demand for loyalty to the crown, Gavin's plight still tugged at her heartstrings, the tie of blood claiming precedence over every other consideration.

'Then it appears I have no option but to tender my resignation.' She trembled back into her chair and clasped her hands over suddenly shaking knees, wondering if she had merely spoken her thoughts aloud or if she really had flung the gauntlet at her boss's motionless feet.

His was the first voice to break the stunned

silence. Sadly, he sighed. 'I would ask you to reconsider that decision, my dear, were it not that I suspect that the same obsessive dedication you've devoted to your career has also been lavished upon those fortunate to have gained your love. I shall accept your resignation,' he decided gravely, 'unwillingly, regretfully, yet nevertheless glad to be relieved of the enormous worry that one of my staff might be provoked into a course of action that could have serious repercussions. As a private individual, you can feel free to explore any avenue that may lead to your brother's release.'

Her scared blue eyes followed his progress towards a paper-strewn desk and remained fixed while he rummaged through drawers, then finally pounced upon a slim leather-bound address book, with a grunt of approval. Seconds later he slipped a scrap of paper into her nerveless fingers.

'I shouldn't be doing this,' he admitted gruffly, 'but because I admire your pluck, and trust you to be discreet enough to keep my name out of any subsequent conversation, I feel I must give you what little help I can. It's the address of the only man known to me who possesses sufficient authority to overrule the charge that has been brought against your brother—a government Minister, Stelios Heracles. If you're lucky, you may find him in residence at his home, Buffavento Castle, situated somewhere on the heights of Cyprus's Mount Olympus.'

CHAPTER TWO

LARNACA airport was teeming with tourists. Three passenger aircraft had landed within minutes of each other, and as Petra withstood the crush inside the Customs hall, dawdling at the end of a long, long queue, she was struck for the very first time—in spite of many previous visits to Cyprus—by the brusque manners and grim expressions of Customs officials and by the intimidating stature of policemen with gunbelts slung low upon their hips, patrolling the perimeter of the crowd.

During a succession of happy holidays spent in the company of parents who had met and married on the 'Island of Love', the supposed birthplace of the goddess Aphrodite, she had had no cause for fear, no reason to delve beneath the surface of sparkling blue sea; long, seemingly endless beaches; everlasting sunshine; the mind-dizzying music of lyra, tambourine, dulcimer; and the incredibly generous hospitality, in search of the hardcore characteristics of a race which for centuries had fought off hordes of invaders, inspired during their struggle for independence by the battle cry: Freedom or Death . . .!

When the airport formalities had finally been completed she lugged her suitcase outside the building, feeling sweat trickling between her shoulderblades as she approached a line of waiting taxis. Gratefully she handed over her burden to an eager young driver before diving into the back of the cab to close her eyes against the glare of brilliant sunshine.

'Police headquarters, Larnaca, if you please,' she instructed fluently in a tongue learnt at her mother's knee.

The driver's astonishment struck her as ludicrous, but she shrank back into a corner of the cab and once more closed her eyes, intending to rehearse the approach she would make, the arguments and pleas that were frighteningly imminent.

But the cheerfully grinning driver apparently felt duty bound to entertain his passenger. Immediately the ignition was switched on the radio started blaring and throughout the entire journey Petra was bombarded with snatches of song and witty conversation tossed across his shoulder while he drove, shouting greetings to other taxi drivers, cursing, and even lifting both hands from the steering wheel to make menacing gestures to other motorists. Concentration was impossible, so much so that she was reduced to saying prayers beneath her breath, placing her trust in the hands of Divine Providence when it became apparent that safety was the last thought in the driver's mind.

She was still shaking when she was shown into the office of a police official whose response to her request to be allowed to see her brother was blank and noncommittal.

'You have written permission to visit the prisoner?'

'No, but——'

'Then I'm sorry, *thespinis*, but unless you have a

letter authorising such a visit your request cannot be granted.'

'But you *must* let me see him—I've come all the way from England! In any case,' she flared, forgetting all her diplomatic training, 'you have no right to hold him here—my brother is innocent, he wouldn't dream of committing such an offence!'

'I'm sorry.' She backed away in alarm when the official loomed menacingly, then choked back a gasp of relief when she realised that he was merely anxious to show her to the door. 'Please go now,' he ordered with steely politeness. 'Come back with a letter or not at all.'

The thought of Gavin being so near and yet so far, confined somewhere within the depths of the same austere building as herself, prompted an act of desperation. Because of Sir Joseph's reluctance to become involved she had decided against following up his suggestion, nevertheless she found herself blurting to the grim, unco-operative official.

'Then can you tell me where I might get in touch with Stelios Heracles?'

The man's eyes narrowed. Though his expression remained wooden, his tone sounded much less peremptory.

'You are acquainted with the Minister?'

'Yes,' she lied recklessly, 'we're very good friends. It was he who begged me to look him up if ever I visited Cyprus.'

She saw a flash of uncertainty in the official's eyes, followed by a cloud of doubt. Then, much to her palm-damp, weak-kneed relief, he decided to err on the side of caution by giving her the benefit of the doubt.

'At this moment,' he glanced at a wall clock, 'the Minister will no doubt be busy with his affairs in Nicosia, where all government offices are situated.'

'Good,' she bluffed. 'I'll call a taxi.'

'That will not be necessary.' To her dismay, he blocked her exit with a detaining arm. 'I will be happy to provide you with transport and also with an escort who will be instructed to remain with you until he is satisfied,' his smile exuded hidden menace, 'that you have been received by the Minister and that, consequently, transport will not be required for your return journey!'

Nursing the very definite impression that she might be in danger of being prosecuted for deliberately wasting police time, Petra sat huddled like a prisoner in the back seat of the police car, her mouth parched as the eternal dust rising from dunes spread like powdered cement along the highway. In less than an hour her bluff would be called and she would be ignominiously returned to face the implacable, steely-eyed official who she sensed would not hesitate to extract some vengeful punishment for her impulsive lie.

Feverish thoughts had rendered her blind to her surroundings—so much so that her heart reacted with a leap of trepidation when the speeding car slowed down to a crawl. The driver had begun negotiating the narrow streets of a sprawling, untidy capital—part of an old city that seemed soaked with the atmosphere of an Eastern bazaar, a place where camels had trodden cobbled streets lined with old houses, flower-filled courtyards, and balconies almost meeting overhead; where dark, cavernous shops had stocked everything from animal feed to incense; where the sound of many hammers had risen in the air while silver and coppersmiths sat crosslegged on the ground fashioning articles of their trade.

When they emerged from the labyrinth the car picked up speed. Petra spotted a green oasis of parkland bordered with palm trees, a shimmering lake and a variety of ornamental shrubs before the car was braked to a standstill outside of a modern building where a ceramic mural decorated with actors' masks seemed to indicate a theatrical connection.

Her escort soon disabused her of this notion. Sternly, obviously determined to carry out orders to be polite, he opened the rear door and indicated that he wished her to alight.

'The House of Representatives,' he pointed proudly. 'Admission to members of the public is forbidden, but if you would please accompany me into the foyer I will ensure that the Minister is informed of your presence.'

She felt his grip upon her arm and wondered if he could sense her inward quaking, whether his grim smile had resulted from his awareness of her frantic mental scrabbling for some magic password that might gain her entry into the office of the man who had chosen to live in close proximity to gods who reputedly resided upon the heights of Mount Olympus.

Her guard, as she had mentally tabbed him, did not relax his grip until they had been shown into a reception room where they were asked to state their business.

'Well, *thespinis*,' he smiled thinly at Petra, 'what message of introduction would you like to have sent to your friend the Minister?'

Desperation caught her by the throat. She felt pinned, cornered, so like a condemned prisoner within sight of the gallows, decided she had nothing to lose by gambling all on one last defiant act of bravado.

Unconsciously adopting the attitude of quiet authority that had been expected of a senior diplomat's secretary, she withdrew a notebook and pen from her handbag and scribbled a few terse words on a blank page.

Minister, I have an important message from a mutual friend which can only be delivered verbally.

Carefully she folded the note and handed it over, praying that the sceptical policeman was unable to translate from English. Then she sank down upon a chair to wait, preparing herself mentally for the ministerial dismissal that would undoubtedly seal her doom.

When the receptionist returned less than five fraught minutes later, Petra found it hard to decide who was the most surprised, herself or her police escort, by the response to her note.

'The Minister will see you immediately, *thespinis*. Please follow me, I'll show you the way to his office.'

Too stunned even to cast a look of triumph in the direction of the obviously nonplussed policeman, Petra trembled to her feet and was guided along passageways lined with offices bustling with activity and resounding with the clattering of typewriters, into a lift that swooshed upwards to a level of silent corridors carpeted to deaden every footfall and lined with doors each bearing an impressive brass plate denoting the name and status of the occupant.

Her thumping heart reacted with a lessening of tension to familiar surroundings, to the atmosphere of a calm, unhurried efficiency in which she had spent most of her working life. All ministers with whom she had come into contact, she consoled herself, had been kindly, elderly gentlemen possessing impeccable manners and having a tendency to treat all members of the opposite sex with charming, old-world courtesy. Stelios Heracles would be no different from the rest, she was assuring herself firmly as she stepped inside a lofty, book-lined room that could have accommodated an entire cabinet of ministers yet did not manage to diminish the dominating stature of the man who rose from his seat behind a paper-strewn desk.

'*Kalispera, thespinis . . .!*' He broke off, then as if a glance at the note he was holding had reminded him that she was English, he abandoned the Greek greeting. 'How do you do, Miss . . .?'

The quirk of a black, enquiring eyebrow prompted her to respond.

'Morrison. Petra Morrison.'

'Please sit down, Miss Morrison.' He waved her towards a leather-covered armchair placed strategically so that she was positioned directly within his sights when he resumed his seat behind the imposing desk.

'Curiosity, one of my many vices, forbids me to leave anything doubtful and undecided,' he explained gravely, 'which is why, in spite of the fact that I am overburdened with work that must be completed before the summer recess, I could not wait to be informed about the important message you are carrying from a mutual friend.'

His manner was courteous, but the hint of impatience tinting his words called for a prompt explanation of her intrusion into urgent business affairs.

Yet all she could do was stare dumbly, feeling completely dominated by the height and athletic physique of the man whose profile was as familiar to her as the moulded features of a statuette that was her grandfather's most cherished possession—the blade-straight nose with flared nostrils; unsmiling mouth with a full, sensuous bottom lip direct gaze, broad brow, and thick black mane of hair peculiar to Heracles, the hero worshipped throughout Greece as the personification of physical strength and as the protector and counsellor of men. A hero who was purported to have lain in wait in the house of a king for the arrival of a ferocious lion and exercised his virility meantime by lying in a single night with his host's fifty daughters. Heracles—the mighty—Hercules . . .!

'Well, Miss Morrison . . .?' Pointedly, he glanced at his watch, rearing on a leash of impatience. 'I'm sorry to have to hurry you, but I have very little time to spare. What message do you have for me, and what is the name of our mutual friend?'

Petra gasped, jolted back to earth from a world of myth and fantasy.

'I . . . I can't tell you his name,' she stammered. 'For reasons impossible to explain at this moment, he has to remain anonymous. But believe me, he really does exist, and he is as anxious as I am to prevent a serious miscarriage of justice.'

When he muttered an imprecation and rose to stride around the desk towards her, she felt she knew exactly how the early Christians must have felt when the first bloodthirsty lion padded into the arena.

'I am beginning to suspect,' he confided in a menacing growl that sent a shiver chasing down the length of her spine, 'that our mutual friend is a figment of your imagination! Do you make a practice of lying to gain entry into places that are forbidden to you, Miss Morrison?'

In spite of a consciences arguing that his anger was justified, she reacted with a flare of temper to the accusation.

'I'd find no necessity to lie to *reasonable* people, but you Greeks are so implacable, so swift to condemn and punish, so deaf to argument! For almost two days now my brother has been locked up inside one of your jails, accused of trying to smuggle drugs into the country! Yet he's guilty only of being the victim of a practical joker, a fellow university student whose high spirits and misguided sense of humour led him to plant a few reefer cigarette ends in my brother's pocket during a boisterous end-of-term party. My brother can be a little irresponsible at times, I must admit, but he is not addicted to drugs, nor would he ever dream of handling the filthy stuff!' She glared, resisting a temptation to stamp her foot with rage. 'But your policemen refused to listen to reason, won't even allow him to be visited by me, his sister, the person responsible for his welfare!'

Stelios Heracles' thick black eyebrows winged high towards his furrowed brow.

'What age is your brother, Miss Morrison?' he snapped.

'Almost nineteen.'

'Old enough to be conscripted into the armed forces; old enough to be eligible to vote, and to be considered mature enough to marry and raise a family of his own. Yet apparently he willingly allows a woman to accept responsibility for his actions!'

'I'm all the family he has,' she faltered, resenting the glint of contempt in his dark eyes. 'Since the loss of our parents, Gavin has tended to look to me for guidance. Boys don't become men overnight. Given time, he will mature into a sensible, caring adult . . .'

'Greek men are men when they emerge from their mothers' wombs,' he condemned coldly. 'Perhaps your brother's progress towards maturity might have been accelerated had he not been hampered by a sister's selfish need to have someone to mother, some dependant whose love had to compensate for the lack of a husband and for the status of motherhood that all women yearn to achieve!'

She shrank back feeling cowed, oppressed by the weight of his shadow as he bent nearer to stress:

'Obsessional love is a dangerous self-indulgence, Miss Morrison—it deprives one of pride, of intellect, even of firmly rooted principles that have to be sacrificed without a qualm in order to protect the object of one's affections. Women who nurture that kind of passion are selfish in the extreme. The needs of their victim are not their primary consideration, they are concerned only with their own needs. The object of their obsession is allowed no flaws because such love demands perfection. It is obvious, from what little I've seen of you, *thespinis*, that what you need most is a husband and a brood of adoring children to mop up and spread around your abundance of potentially dangerous devotion. And what is equally obvious is your brother's urgent need of space—space to mature, to develop his own personality!'

Petra sat as if rooted, her eyes stormy with outrage, reduced for the first time in her life to speechless anger. Her late colleagues would have found difficulty in recognising the girl who eventually trembled to her feet, so seething with passionate resentment she was barely able to croak:

'Have you quite finished analysing my character?'

He nodded, looking quite unperturbed. 'For the moment, yes. However,' he frowned, 'I feel obliged to investigate your accusation of injustice. My enquiries will take time. Have you some place to stay?'

Petra's heart should have soared with triumph, but instead it slowly sank. Because of Gavin's many demands she had found it impossible to save any of her better-than-average salary. What little money she had left would be needed to tide them over until she found another job, therefore booking into a hotel was out of the question. The most obvious place for her to stay was her grandfather's home, situated in a village on the slopes of the Troodos mountains, but dared she risk living in the shadow of Buffavento Castle, the home of the Minister who was almost certain to have recruited staff from nearby villages that were hotbeds of rural gossip? Dared she take the admittedly slim risk of some member of the castle staff being acquainted with her grand-father? In spite of his inability to comprehend how it had been allowed to happen, she was aware that her grandfather boasted non-stop to his cronies about the exceptional intelligence that had gained his English granddaughter entry into the male-dominated Diplomatic Corps. Stelios Heracles, she reluctantly conceded, would be quicker than most to put two and two together, to listen, conjecture, and finally to bracket her with Sir Joseph, who had made plain his reluctance to become even remotely involved in Gavin's misfortune.

'No,' she jerked, ashamed of being forced to lie once more, 'I did not come prepared for a long stay.'

Predictably, his intimidating eyebrows rose. 'Why not? Did you imagine that your brother's release could easily be bought with persuasive argument? Or perhaps you envisaged a squad of Greek policemen falling immediate victims to the appeal of your incredibly blue eyes?'

She blushed deeply, avoiding his mocking glance as she struggled to decide whether to grimace at the bitterness of the pill he had doled or to savour its sugar-coated sweetness.

She had no way of knowing how tired and defeated she appeared to the man used to venting his anger upon men who did not hesitate to return spleen with spleen, scowl with scowl, curse with rumbustious curse. Consequently, the gentleness of his tone caused her a shock of pleasure.

'Are you prepared to work for your keep, Miss Morrison?'

She looked up, her expression hopeful, her eyes wide with wonder.

'Yes, of course...' She nodded affirmation when a breath clogged her throat.

He nodded approval, then casually, displaying the sensuous assurance of a king of beasts, he returned to the carved, high-backed chair rising stately as a throne behind an equally imposing desk.

'What sort of work are you trained to do?' His mouth twisted into an ironic smile. 'At a guess, I'd say you are either a teacher, a nurse, or a social worker.'

Gratefully, Petra snatched the first straw he had tossed her way.

'I'm a teacher,' she gasped, swallowing hard to suppress an impulse to confess that she was also fast becoming an accomplished liar.

'Good!' Do you specialise in any particular subject?'

'L-languages,' she stammered, opting for safety, bolstered by the knowledge that her Greek was excellent and that at one stage in her education she had considered working for a degree in Classics. 'I can teach Greek, Latin, and English, of course.'

He had been doodling idly on a jotter, but at this admission his head jerked up to train a glance of keen interest.

'You understand our language well enough to teach?'

She nodded, uplifted by his obvious incredulity. 'I do.'

'In that case, Miss Morrison, the problem of finding you work can be considered solved. Our children are not allowed to emulate the example of your brother and his fellow students who appear to favour spending their summer break lazing under the tree of idleness. Because all Greek-Cypriot parents like to boast that their children can speak and understand English well, tutors are employed to supply extra instruction outside normal school hours. However, temporary teachers are hard to find, which is why I can promise that your services will be very much appreciated by both parents and pupils of the small village school attached to my Troodos estate. I shall, of course, be pleased to offer you accommodation in my home for the duration of your employment.'

He had spoken as if her acceptance of his proposition was a foregone conclusion. She longed to spurn his offer with a show of open distaste, but the reminder of the police escort waiting downstairs to pounce, together with the blessed relief of having all her expenses paid for as long as it took to obtain Gavin's release, caused her to hesitate.

'What about my brother?' she husked, unconsciously pleading. 'If I were to accept the post, would you be prepared to guarantee his early release?'

'I can promise you nothing!' he bit, bridling

with impatience. 'You ought to consider yourself fortunate to have been offered a way out of your financial difficulties. My advice to you, Miss Morrison,' his upper lip curled, 'is to reach out with grateful hands and grab what little the gods seem prepared to offer!'

CHAPTER THREE

AFTER the heat of the capital the air in the mountains fell like a cool caress against Petra's hot cheeks while she was being driven in an open-topped car along dirt roads curving upwards from the foothills towards pine tree forests. She caught glimpses on the way of villages nestling in valleys; clinging in layers to steep hillsides, saw the rooftops of ancient monasteries hiding behind trees, and streams glistening like silver ribbons cascading from unseen heights.

An occasional lorry passed them on its way to the local winery where, later in the year, grapes slowly ripening in dozens of small vineyards would be collected and crushed into Cypriot Nana, the wine Cypriots swore was so ancient it had been consumed in great quantities at the springtime festivals of Aphrodite.

She wriggled deeper into her seat to enjoy sights familiar from childhood, landscape that had remained unchanged for centuries yet which constantly presented aspects that were thrilling, beautiful, and new. Idly she played with the collar of her blouse, easing it aside so that refreshing fingers of breeze could venture within pale hollows and warm curves secreted behind crumpled, classically tailored poplin. Eyes that seemed capable of dissecting every gesture and emotion immediately spotted the small sign of discomfort.

36

'Do you always wear such ... er ... sensible clothes, Miss Morrison?'

She stiffened, resenting the impudent quirk of lips struggling to suppress a grin of amusement, too proud to point out that financial circumstances had denied her the pleasure of indulging in frivolous dresses that would have looked completely out of place in an office.

'Most girls of my acquaintance,' he continued casually, 'abandon all constricting clothing at the first sign of spring, thereby supplying members of my own sex with the seasonal treat of watching their emergence from winter cocoons to flaunt as freely as butterflies flaunt colourful, transparent wings. It seems a pity,' he increased her aggravation with a mocking sideways glance, 'that one endowed with a body as shapely as yours should go to so much trouble to hide it! I'm certain modern-minded pupils would form a closer affinity to a youthfully uninhibited teacher than they would to one who clings to prudish mores that were fashionable during your Queen Victoria's reign.'

Petra bit her lip, determined not to be riled into reckless speech by the man who seemed to take perverse pleasure in prompting signs of embarrassment, of goading her into a rise of colour so that he could stare as if fascinated by some curious phenomenon, a message of modesty expressed in some ancient forgotten language. But in spite of the bite of determined teeth, her bottom lip quivered as she asked herself what could possibly be wrong with her image to cause a man of such short acquaintance to decide that she was prim and proper, to confirm, in fact, the aptness of the hurtful title that had been bestowed by office juniors.

'What is it about me that compels even complete strangers to label me "Miss Grundy",' she burst out impulsively, then wanted to bite off a tongue that had betrayed the weakness of her defences to an enemy.

Fractionally, the car swerved off course. He regained control immediately, yet sounded apologetic, almost pitying, when quietly he assured her:

'It was not my intention to hurt your feelings, Miss Morrison—to tease a little, perhaps, but not to condemn a quality of solemn repose so treasured by the Moslem race they have coined for it a special word. *Kayf*—an easy silence, not meditation or daydreaming but something much more profound, a fathomless peace that demands nothing that a companion is not prepared to give, neither wit nor wisdom, questions nor answers.'

He waited until the road was running straight as an arrow through an avenue of trees before casting an enquiring glance, but when her only response was a deepening blush he dispersed what was threatening to become an embarrassing silence by briskly changing the subject.

'Tell me, where in Cyprus had your brother arranged to stay for the duration of his holiday? As a student he is hardly likely to be able to afford the prices charged by popular seaside hotels.'

Involuntarily, Petra's fingers clenched around the rim of her handbag. Conversation with Stelios Heracles was comparable with negotiating a path through a treacherous bog—one moment she felt encouraged by the firmness of the ground beneath her feet, the next she was floundering in a morass of lies and deceit!

'Gavin hadn't planned to stay long in any particular place,' she blurted when his puzzlement of her silence grew obvious. Then, recalling with relief a chance remark her brother had once made, she elaborated in a panic: 'It was his intention to tour the mountain villages, staying no longer than a couple of days in each. Far from being prepared to idle away his time, as you suggested, he came to Cyprus in search of first-hand knowledge of the subject of a thesis he has chosen to undertake concerning the manners and customs of Greek-Cypriot peasants and the way they live their lives.'

Her heartbeats quickened when dark eyes swivelled a look that seemed to imply that for once something she had said had aroused the interest and approval of the too-youthful, too modern-minded, too blatantly virile Minister who was the complete antithesis of others she had known. Optimism about Gavin's prospects of release rose still higher when he mused thoughtfully:

'The subject your brother has chosen to research is one that is very near to my own heart. For some time now I have been toying with the idea of engaging someone interested and able enough to chronicle the everyday doings of people who have resisted change for centuries. The villagers on my estate must be some of the few remaining who still insist upon using a distaff for spinning cotton and wool; who use a pestle and mortar to pound spices; who spin their own silk, weave their own cloth, make their own saddles, and bake bread in a communal oven. Sooner or later, without their being aware of it, civilisation will encroach even the lofty heights of Mount Olympus,' he brooded, heaving an unconscious sigh of regret. 'Unless someone takes the trouble to record for posterity manners and customs unique to this land, they will be allowed to fade away, become lost in the mists of history. Do you know, Miss Morrison,' he emerged from his absorption to confide with a grin, 'fathers of some village girls still insist upon exercising their prerogative to set any prospective son-in-law a test of strength. Traditionally, the young man is asked to chop a tree trunk into planks with an axe, and to make his task even harder the tree trunk chosen is usually an oak that has been left soaking in the river for forty days! Fortunately, though, one custom that has been allowed to lapse is that of parents arranging marriages for their children. These days, it is not quite so common for a couple in love to find themselves married to two other people.'

When he fell silent to concentrate all his attention upon negotiating the purring limousine around a particularly awkward bend, Petra sat quietly, clasping her hands together in an effort to still their trembling, striving to remain rational, reminding herself that as yet there was no specific reason why optimism should be allowed to soar as high as the trills of a pair of feathered siskins who were engaging in a flirtatious dance as they circled above the trees.

Then without prior warning the symmetry of the landscape became broken by huge boulders, an avalanche of stones which some time in antiquity must have cascaded from the heights of Mount Olympus. She leant sideways, craning her neck to follow the progress of rocks laying a petrified trail down the sloping sides of a valley towards a collection of dwellings, their ancient roofs joined together, making it possible to take a rooftop walk from one end of a street to the other.

'The village of Sabri,' Stelios Heracles nodded briefly, 'a place where the majority of your future pupils live in houses built as solidly as the boulders utilised long ago to form their foundations. One particularly large stone that marks the entrance to the village has been named the "coupling stone" because for as long as anyone can remember it has been the custom for newlyweds to walk around it immediately after the wedding ceremony and to whisper a wish that their love will remain as strong and steady as the stone. *Petra tou Androginou*— "Stone of the Couple",' he translated unnecessarily, then smiled with secret amusement.

'It is to be hoped that the children who are to be handed into your care will have no cause to complain about a teacher whose nature can be as crushing and implacable as her name, Miss *Petra* Morrison!' The stress he placed, though light, held an unmistakable ring of warning.

'I hope so too,' she agreed, striving to maintain an even tone and somehow succeeding, in spite of a heart that reacted with a quiver to every hurtful remark. Then, prompted by an uncharacteristic urge to retaliate, she continued with more than a hint of asperity:

'However, if a choice of name is to be deemed a fair indication of its owner's character, surely I'm the one most entitled to feel misgivings. It's less than two hours since you and I first met, yet I have allowed myself to be driven up into the mountains where I'm to reside for weeks in the lair of a man whose namesake, Heracles, became synonymous with lust and fertility when the fifty daughters of Thestius all conceived a child by him in one night!'

She felt her brazen retort had been justified when for long, satisfactory seconds he looked astounded. Then suddenly his dark features dissolved into lines of amusement as he tossed back his head and laughed loudly enough to dislodge a disgruntled hen-bird from her nest.

'Truly, you are an enigma, Miss Morrison!' he finally gasped, controlling his amusement long enough to assure her. 'You possess qualities as secret and impossible to define as the coupling stone whose character changes according to the play of light. Familiarity has long since condemned it as mundane, yet sometimes in the evening I have been surprised by its beauty, being made suddenly aware of it in a way that I would have considered practically impossible during less receptive daylight hours.'

As they left the village behind the road grew steeper, the landscape became harshened by a vista of craggy peaks and outcrops of rock that jutted from the roadside causing many blind corners on the road rising narrow and almost perpendicular towards the lonely, lofty territory of the gods. When the car breasted a steep rise, then suddenly dipped, a gasp of wonder escaped Petra's lips. Her startled eyes widened as she gazed down upon a desolate hollow where the evening sun did not penetrate through the narrow, fortified windows of an ancient castle of pitted yellow stone lying, soaking in shadows, by tier upon tier of towering cypress trees. The silence was uncanny, it was a place where no birds sang, a kingdom of shadows, she decided with a shudder, where the souls of those who had finished their earthly existence might look for refuge.

As the car approached the castle drive her optimism faded as quickly as the warmth of sunrays that had played around her thinly-clad shoulders. She shivered, feeling a chill of foreboding, faced by the full extent of the folly of having allowed herself to be spirited into the primitive past, to a place where time had obviously stood still, by a stranger whose words flowed like honey from a spoon!

'Buffavento Castle,' he indicated with evident satisfaction as they drove past huge bronze gates, each with a centrepiece of a shield stamped with the image of a lion rampant, guarding the entrance to his stronghold. 'Or perhaps you prefer the title said to have been coined by Richard the Lionheart, your crusading king who needed to rest between battles inside an impregnable fortress— Castle of the Lion!'

Lair might be a more apt description, Petra decided, nervously eyeing a flight of stone steps hollowed by the advancing feet of many centuries; pitted, battle scarred walls; slit-narrow window embrasures, and turrets sited high enough to enable a lookout to provide early warning of approaching enemies.

By the time she had been ushered inside a huge hall hung with brass lanterns and dusty banners, its floor dotted with uninhabited chairs and rugs spilling a few pools of bright colour on to a chilly stone-flagged floor, her chilled blood had developed a definite hint of ice. Conscious of his amused eyes reading her expression, she faltered to a standstill in the middle of the hall, wincing as if expecting to be trampled by Herculean footsteps when he strode past to tug a bell rope dangling against one wall.

Seconds later, as if her presence had been summoned in a deliberate attempt to disperse fear and childish apprehension, a woman bustled smartly into the hall, a plump, rather elderly woman wearing a spotless white apron over a dress black as her smoothly-brushed hair, fastened at the neck with small jet buttons reflecting the same bright, friendly sparkle as her eyes.

'Miss Morrison,' Stelios Heracles turned, 'I'd like to introduce Sophia, my housekeeper.

'Sophia,' he addressed the beaming woman, 'Miss Morrison will be staying with us for a few weeks. I shall rely upon you to ensure that everything necessary for her comfort will be provided. Though our guest is English,' he encouraged when he saw Sophia's look of apprehension, 'she is sufficiently familiar with our language to have accepted the post of temporary English teacher to the children of the village. So you see, there is no need for you to worry about communicating with our guest.'

'Ah! *Kopiaste, thespinis.*' Alternately bobbing

and beaming, Sophia invited: 'Come, sit, and let us talk.'

'*Efharisto*, Sophia,' Petra thanked her shyly, guessing from past experience of Greek hospitality that she was about to be shown into the most comfortable room and plied with coffee and 'sweets of the spoon'—hospitality which custom demanded should be extended immediately any visitor entered a Greek home.

As she had anticipated, shortly after being shown into a magnificently proportioned sitting-room where modern items of furniture blended inconspicuously with heavily carved chests blackened with age, delicate porcelain, gilt-framed oil paintings, and a magnificent crystal chandelier, Sophia reappeared carrying a large silver tray set with glasses, tiny spoons, and numerous bowls of *glyko*—a variety of fruits, green walnuts, small egg plants, citrus peel and rose blossoms preserved in thick, sweet syrup. Eager to participate in a ritual described many times by her mother, Petra leant forward in her chair to accept a glass of water and a spoon which she used to scoop out of one of the bowls a large, glossy cherry. She then transported it to her lips, using the glass of water to catch syrup dripping from the spoon.

'*Iyenete!*' Sophia nodded approval of her dexterity.

'*Efharisto,*' Petra thanked her, 'that was delicious.' She ran the tip of an appreciative tongue around syrup-sweetened lips. 'Do you make your own confiture?'

'But of course!' Sophia looked astonished. 'Every good housewife makes her own *glyko* as well as her jams and marmalades. The art was taught to me by my mother, who had the method handed down to her by her mother, and her mother, and her mother before that! No recipe book can describe fruit that is exactly right—not too ripe and not too green—how to get the thickness of the syrup just so. This kind of knowledge can only be gained by watching an expert at work.' She bent to put a light to a silver spirit stove. 'And now, *thespinis*, please tell me how you like your coffee. The *kyrios* prefers his bitter with no sugar at all . . .'

'Then that will suit me too,' Petra told her hastily, aware of the complicated ritual that was about to ensue, 'but with just a little water poured into it to disperse the froth.'

'*Kalos orisate,*' Sophia acknowledged her thoughtfulness, then began measuring heaped spoonsful of coffee into an *imbriki* containing heated water before putting the pot back on to the spirit heater to allow the liquid to bubble and rise to the brim.

'Remember not to drain your cup,' she warned, pouring the aromatic brew into tiny cups. 'You will find the thick sediment at the bottom comes in very useful when fortunes are being told.'

Petra rewarded the caution with a smile, feeling contented and happy as memories resurrected from childhood flooded her mind. But pleasure turned to shock when she looked up to encounter the narrow-eyed stare of the man whose still, watchful presence had barely impinged upon her consciousness.

'You appear to be as knowledgeable about our

customs as you are about our language, Miss Morrison.' Stelios Heracles sounded almost accusing. 'I've lost count of the number of times I've been called upon to explain to foreign visitors, when confronted for the very first time with offerings of *glyko,* that one is not expected to eat a dishful, but merely to sweeten a friendship with the contents of a spoon. Would I be correct in assuming that you are no stranger to my country?'

Carefully, Petra transferred her fragile coffee cup on to a nearby table, making her actions deliberately slow so as to give her flustered thoughts time to settle, to give her mind time to click into the smooth calm groove she sought whenever she was faced with a difficult situation. To admit that her mother had been one of his own countrywomen, an exile who had returned each year with her family to the mountain village where she had been born, would be to invite the inevitable enquiry about relatives. To Greeks, the preservation of family ties was of primary importance. Cousins, half-cousins, even distant relatives whose connections were so slight as to be barely worth mentioning were never allowed to lose touch, and however far distant they might live, were invited and expected to attend every event that called for a family gathering.

So it would be useless to protest that she had no relatives on the island to whom she could have turned for shelter. Neither could she continue to protect the grandfather whose fierce Greek pride would be outraged if ever he should discover the shame that his grandson had inadvertently inflicted upon his family.

She chanced a glance from under lowered lashes and saw that her inquisitor was becoming impatient. Forced to abandon caution, she mumbled:

'My mother was Greek.'

She tensed, anticipated a spate of questions about her mother's exact place of birth, then had to struggle to suppress a blush of shame when, taking her honesty and integrity for granted, he responded lightly:

'Ah, that explains a lot! Some of our local customs are peculiar to Cyprus, but many are traditionally Greek and practised on the mainland as well as throughout the islands.'

In one sleek, supple movement he rose to his feet, looking pleasantly satisfied.

'I must apologise for being unable to join you for dinner this evening, Miss Morrison. Officially, I've begun my vacation and will not be expected to appear in my office for some weeks yet. However,' she read a hint of weariness in his sigh and in the distracted way his fingers raked across his scalp, ruffling a black fleece of hair into disarray, 'as a great deal of work has been left undone, I shall be forced to spend part of each day in my study attempting to clear the backlog. I intend working late this evening so that tomorrow I will have time to spare to take you to meet your pupils.'

'Is it absolutely necessary for you to effect the introduction?' she protested, sympathetic to the sort of pressure she knew well. 'Couldn't someone else accompany me—your wife, perhaps?'

'I have no wife,' he responded smoothly. 'It has

long been my belief that no pleasure can endure unless seasoned by variety.'

Her heart leapt, jolted by the shock of discovering a situation she had never once envisaged. She stared, her stunned eyes questioning his right to compromise her reputation in a way that one of his own countrywomen would have found unforgiveable.

'Then how dared you bring me here!' she croaked. 'I would never have dreamt of accepting your invitation had I known——'

'Certainly you would, Miss Morrison! As you have already ably demonstrated by tricking your way into my office, one who lives as selfishly and possessively as yourself does not hesitate to kick down any barrier of scruples separating her from a loved one. In any case, English girls are notoriously lax in their efforts to maintain an aura of innocence. They come to our island in search of sun and the sort of excitement that is to be found in laying an enticing trail for a susceptible Greek male who reacts with the instincts of a hunter, then eventually discovers himself trapped, cornered by a sharp-clawed, predatory Bambi!'

Indolently, he began strolling towards the door, showing not the slightest sign of repentance, then paused to mock hatefully:

'I'm sorry to have to disappoint you, but amorous *Miss Grundys* hold no appeal for me. Consequently, I can offer no hope at all of your ever being called upon to share the same glorious fate as King Thestius's fifty virgin daughters!'

CHAPTER FOUR

MUCH to her surprise, Petra slept well. She was awakened the following morning by a choir of birds trilling an appreciative anthem to a sun already risen high enough to penetrate the partially open slats of window shutters, creating an impression in her sleep-befuddled mind of being held captive, imprisoned within a cell with bars of sparkling gold.

She was only just becoming acclimatised to her strange new surroundings when a tap upon the bedroom door preceded Sophia's entry into the room.

'*Kalimera, thespinis!*' she beamed, bustling forward to set a laden breakfast tray upon a convenient table. 'I hope you found your bed comfortable?'

'I certainly did.' Petra levered herself into a sitting position, struggling to suppress a yawn. 'In fact, it's almost too comfortable, I'm still only half awake. Usually, I'm an early riser—I certainly had no intention of putting you to the trouble of serving breakfast in my room.'

'*Trouble?*' Petra was amused when Sophia communicated amazement in a manner that was typically Greek and probably older than language itself by raising her eyebrows, rolling her eyes upwards, throwing her head back and at the same time raising both hands in the air. 'I never find my duties troublesome—on the contrary, I look forward to the times when the *kyrios* brings guests to stay and especially enjoy looking after those who are as young and pretty as yourself, *thespinis*. I keep hoping,' she sighed with an enquiring pathos that made Petra feel even more inclined to smile, 'that some day soon the *kyrios* will introduce me to his future wife. Like all Greek men he cherishes his freedom, but,' her mouth pursed, yet an attempt to look severe was spoiled by a twinkle that betrayed the pride and fondness she felt for her employer, 'the *kyrios* has enjoyed a larger share of carefree bachelorhood than most men in his position. In spite of his aversion to matrimonial ties he must surely be about ready to accept the burden of duty that calls for a son to carry on his name, to inherit the castle and estate that has been in the possession of the Heracles family for centuries.'

Vigorously, as if feeling a need to vent her frustration on some inanimate object, she pummelled a pillow before offering it to Petra as a backrest.

'He is a handsome devil, don't you think?'

Petra avoided her hopeful look, conscious that she was being expected to praise and flatter, yet unable to think of one complimentary comment to make about the man whose insulting implication that she was incapable of arousing his interest had left her smarting.

'Such a husband he would make!' Sophia enthused, oblivious to any lack of enthusiasm. 'A man born under the sign of strength and light, with a mother who instilled into him a love of beauty, who taught him wisdom and virtue, and a father who bequeathed his superb athletic stature, his readiness to accept a challenge of strength and the restless disposition of an eternal conqueror who can find no repose but waits, always impatiently, for yet another joust, another victory!'

Steadying the tray that had been placed upon her lap, Petra concentrated all her attention on spreading a slice of oven-warm bread with a generous helping of honey. Then, made uneasy by Sophia's expectant stare, she licked the tips of sticky fingers before stating politely:

'You obviously know your employer well. Have you spent long in the service of his family?'

'I worked here long before his mother was brought to Buffavento Castle as a bride,' Sophia preened proudly, obviously eager to begin recounting the family's entire history. 'I assisted at the *kyrios*'s birth; helped to nurse him through all his childhood ailments, and did what I could to console him when the news that both his parents had died in a boating accident was broken to him. Not that he looked to anyone for consolation,' she mused thoughtfully. 'He was only sixteen years old at the time, yet he took the blow as bravely as his father would have wished—with a stoical calmness that caused everyone present to marvel at a boy's courageous shouldering of duties and responsibilities that would have broken the spirit of many an older man!'

Hastily, yet hoping to avoid offending the kind, would-be matchmaker whose only obvious fault was a misguided devotion to her employer, Petra

abandoned her breakfast and cut short Sophia's
confidences by handing her the tray.

'Thank you, Sophia, that was delicious. I wish I
had time to eat more, but arrangements have been
made for a meeting with the parents of my future
pupils. I think the *kyrios* intends setting off early
for the village, so I must start getting ready if the
visit is to be concluded before noon.'

She slid out of a bed made luxirious by sheets
woven and spun—Sophia had proudly informed
her the previous evening—by villagers whose skill
in the art of silk-making had been passed on
through families from generation to generation
since the Byzantine times. Yet in spite of an air of
antiquity shrouding the exterior and the ground
floor rooms of the castle, her bedroom was light,
airy, attractively furnished and equipped with the
luxury of a surprisingly modern bathroom.

She enjoyed a quick shower, then, using a towel
as a bathrobe, padded barefoot into the bedroom
to progress in the manner of a bee in search of
pollen across rugs strewing a flower-patterned
path across polished wooden floorboards. She
depressed the curved brass handle of a wardrobe,
then frowned, displeased by the lack of choice,
colour and comfort being offered by a collection
of clothes hanging sparse and dejected inside the
capacious interior. She sighed, experiencing an
often-felt longing for just one dress bright enough
to lift her spirits, a flimsy creation designed to
emphasise thrusting breasts, slim waist, and
slender, shapely thighs, diaphanous enough to
guide the eye along a creamy slope of shoulder,
then plunge downward into a mysterious depth of

cleavage kept discreetly veiled yet remaining sufficiently exposed to rout the hated Miss Grundy analogy for ever!

'If wishes were horses even beggars would ride,' she reminded herself in a wry murmur, reaching for the pale grey co-ordinating skirt and blouse which, when worn to the office, had achieved an aimed-for aura of smart efficiency. 'In any case, your objective in coming here was to secure Gavin's release, not to become skilled in the art of seduction!'

Nevertheless, fifteen minutes later, while she was drifting silently as a grey-clad, bespectacled, impeccably groomed ghost down a fan-shaped marble staircase, a long-forgotten maxim quoted by a professor to his class of Latin scholars was resurrected from memory to haunt her.

'*Carpe diem!* Enjoy the day, seize the present opportunity, improve the time!'

'That outfit you are wearing looks more formidable than a suit of armour!' Petra stumbled, almost missing her footing, when Stelios Heracles suddenly appeared striding arrogantly as an Olympian god across the hallway. 'And why have you found it necessary to hide your most appealing asset behind ugly spectacles which I'm willing to wager have lenses of plain glass and were designed solely to be used as a prop, an aid to disguise inner inadequacies!'

He waited, completely in command of centre stage, a star performer watching a novice's flustered debut. Immediately Petra reached ground level she whipped off the offending spectacles, feeling belittled, cheapened, glaring her resentment of his ability to assess her motives as easily as she could read newsprint with or without her faked lenses.

'Nothing,' she stormed at his relaxed, hatefully self-assured presence, 'makes a woman feel more like an inadequate sex object than a man saying take off your glasses so that I can see your beautiful blue eyes!'

'Did I say your eyes were beautiful?' he bedevilled, tilting a wicked eyebrow. Then, displaying the satisfaction of a duellist who knows he has drawn blood, he relented kindly: 'I'm sorry. If I did not, then I most certainly should have.' Thrusting his hands deep inside the pockets of casual blue denims he surveyed her thoughtfully, paying careful attention to the wave of wild rose colour flooding her cheeks, and to white teeth digging vexedly into a bottom lip quivering with humiliation. Dark eyes flecked with the tawny glint of a jungle king pinned their quarry with a look akin to pity then, as if goaded by an inbred streak of cruelty impossible to control, he subjected her body to an appraisal so shockingly intimate that every curve, every pore, every quivering nerve, shrank from its brooding caress.

'Petra!' he taunted softly, his need to smile seemingly almost compulsive. 'A little rock for all to lean on! Yet I suspect that basically you are a voluptuary—unawakened, as yet, to sensual pleasure.'

Some deeply buried urge stirred, then reared up inside her, some lost chord responding to the pluck of his deep, warm voice against taut nerve-strings—a frightening desire to experience the harmonious union of extreme virtues: timidity with strength; ignorance with experience; tenderness with wild Greek passion!

Then with the suddenness of water dousing flame she was jolted back to sanity. She gasped, appalled by the direction in which her thoughts had been allowed to stray, then without stopping to think, attempted to exorcise her personal disgust by attacking her smiling tormenter.

'And I suspect that you have lived so long on the lofty heights of Olympus you have begun to think and act not as a mere man bound by the rules of civilised convention, but as an omnipotent deity! Is that the reason, perhaps, why you prefer to live in isolation,' she challenged, 'why you cling to the remnants of an ancient civilisation whose simple-minded, easily-manipulated peasants were responsible for turning mere mortals into gods in the first place?'

His proud head reared, displaying an angry thrust of jaw, eyes cold as the glare of a marble statue.

'I resent the implication that I shun modern society, and object to the slur cast upon local villagers whom you appear to have reduced to the level of primitive savages coerced into adopting myself as headman of their village! Must I contradict your argument by reminding you that I hold a ministerial post in government?' he demanded, obviously incensed, she decided contemptuously, by her lack of deferential awe.

'Such a post is merely an extension of the analogy,' she shrugged, recklessly tilting her honey-gold head until his savage mouth appeared directly within her sights. She quaked in the shadow of a towering frame threatening instant reprisal, yet some devil of long-nurtured vexation drove her to even more dangerous lengths.

'In the jungle of bureaucracy old rituals still flourish. Civil servants, in common with most native tribes, have a secret written, spoken, and sign language that is confined solely to male members of the higher echelons. Myths, rituals and tribal customs practised for hundreds of years determine the trappings of power accorded to a headman—a private washroom is considered obligatory by senior male warriors; venerated male elders may even be issued with a small couch or an up-market limousine. But even in these enlightened days, female members of the tribe are denied such privileges. *Tarzan rules, O.K.!* Wouldn't you say so, Minister?' she scathed, frightened half out of her wits by a scowl black as storm clouds gathering around a majestic peak.

'Women must be kept in their place, certainly,' he iced, stating the sort of theory guaranteed to bring a flash of resentment to her blue eyes, a mutinous tilt to her chin. 'It puzzles me why you should be showing such concern for employees in a situation completely outside of your own province. Schoolteaching is an ideal occupation for females. Might I suggest that you concentrate your attention on the job you have been trained to do instead of coveting the status of higher offices whose burdens are best borne by men of strength and purpose, capable of making calm, unemotional decisions. Such qualities are rarely associated with your sex, as I am sure you will agree, Miss Morrison?'

Petra pulled up sharp, stamping a brake upon an irate rush of words ready to speed from her lips. Much as she would have relished disputing the arguments of an omnipotent, typically chauvinistic Greek, she dared not risk arousing the suspicions of the man who held Gavin's fate in the palm of his hand.

She found it hard to swallow her anger, to appear to bow meekly to his superior intellect, yet her shrug of resignation must have been reasonably convincing, because his scowl gave way to a satisfied smile and a remark so patronising she was forced to grit her teeth.

'In order to win an argument one must start by being right,' he grinned widely. 'Try to remember in future that in an argument with a man a woman always comes off worse, however just a cause she might plead, because the worst female trait is emotionalism, and the test of a man is his ability to cope with it.'

Inwardly seething, yet retaining sufficient control to ignore a remark that would have caused a riot among members of any university debating society, Petra accompanied him outside to a waiting car and slid into the passenger seat, determined to pander to his enormous conceit, until she judged his mood mellow enough to broach the subject of Gavin's release. She did not have to wait long. The sweet taste of victory had rendered him amiable enough, as they drove through scented morning air in the direction of the village, to point out items he considered would be of particular interest to a tourist visiting his island for the very first time.

'Listen,' he murmured, 'can you hear the music of the mountains?' He slowed the car to a standstill to allow her to appreciate fully the way pale green grapes hanging heavy on the vines were contrasting beautifully with a deep green backdrop of forest beyond. 'Melodious birds and incessantly sighing pines blending in perfect harmony,' he continued softly. 'Sometimes, when being confined inside an office becomes unbearable, I close my eyes and take an imaginary trip into these mountains, sniffing the delightfully cool air scented with the tang of pine trees, wild herbs and, in the springtime, the intoxicating perfume of mixed fruit blossoms, cherry, apple, pear, plum and almonds, drifting in a fragrant cloud from fertile valley orchids. When we reach the village you must try some of the nectarian wine that is still being produced exactly as it was centuries ago—untouched by chemicals or mechanical means.'

Casting a last appreciative look across his shoulder, he depressed the accelerator until the car began picking up speed.

'How fortunate you are,' Petra sighed, 'to live on an island that's bathed in brilliant sunshine every day, even during the winter!'

'True,' he nodded, causing a corkscrew of hair to tumble down on to his forehead, 'we take our sunshine so much for granted we are at a loss to know what to do when it rains. Life is disrupted to such an extent that the islanders change any plans they may have made to go out and just wait at home until the shower passes and the sun brings a return to normality. Many of our daily customs are built around the frequency and intensity of the sun—the most obvious being the siesta. That is why I dared not linger too long admiring the view, for if we do not arrive at the village before lunchtime the entire morning will be wasted.'

Shortly afterwards the village appeared in the distance like a beautiful painting framed in poplar green, with bursts of colour cascading from flower tubs propped against ancient walls; lightening dark, cool corners; set upon each step of flights leading up to balconies shaded by vine-covered trellis reaching upwards towards ceramic coloured roofs.

'It is beautiful, don't you think?' Stelios Heracles asked her. 'But wait until you catch the scent of basil rising in the still air from pots placed on every verandah, porch, and windowsill lining village streets designed to accommodate only the width of a donkey cart.'

He braked the car to a standstill next to a huge stone standing like a fortress guarding the entrance to the main street.

'The coupling stone,' he indicated with a nod as courteously he held open a door to assist her out of the car. 'One day,' his lips suddenly tightened, 'I shall be forced by conscience to live up to the custom of perambulating round it with my new wife.'

Petra's sensitive ears caught a hint of resentment, a built-up frustration that was emphasised by his violent slamming of the car door. 'How I regret the passing of the ancient Moorish custom of allowing a man concubines, a selection of beauties chosen to provide pleasure yet living side by side with the wife whose main function was to see to his comfort and to bear his legitimate sons!'

Petra's steps faltered. She swung round to stare, outraged by the utterance of a man whose barbaric outlook was insulting to her sex.

'It's hardly surprising that a man holding such views should be experiencing difficulty in finding a marriage partner!' she countered tartly.

'You are right,' he acknowledged the rebuke with a wide grin, 'no Greek girl would submit to such marital indignity. I have heard, however, that many English couples favour a modernised version of the Moorish system—an "open marriage" in which each partner is free to follow his or her own sexual inclinations without any obvious detriment either to marriage or family life. I should not want that, of course,' he declared with godlike superiority. 'A man's wife should be his own private possession. But the acquisition of a nubile, placid-natured wife who asks no more of a husband than that he should provide her with a home and sire a succession of children upon whom she could lavish an abundance of love would suit me very nicely!'

When he began strolling towards her, Petra retreated a few startled steps away, relaying a frantic message to pounding pulses, assuring a panicking heart that there was no need to feel terrorised by the mild stirring of interest in his thoughtful eyes.

'Here is the kyrios!'

'The kyrios has arrived, and he has brought with him our new teacher!'

The shrill of children's voices dispersed the sense of oppression weighting Petra's spirits. In no time at all she found herself surrounded by a crowd of laughing, bright-eyed children, each eager to be introduced to the rare phenomenon—an English girl who could speak their difficult tongue like a native.

Obediently, they obeyed Stelios Heracles' command to fall into line, then responded one by one when he called out names that could have made up a roll-call of mythical gods and goddesses.

'Athene; Hera; Helios; Selene; Phoebe; Cronos: Minos, and even Zeus—a lively, spindly little boy whose wide grin and dancing eyes seemed to indicate a streak of mischievous fun that promised to be as troublesome as his namesake's thunderbolts.

'Run along now!' he instructed when the last giggling girl had dropped Petra a charming curtsey. 'Inform your parents that we have arrived and will be waiting in the schoolroom to meet them.'

Feeling happier than she had done since her arrival in Cyprus, Petra fell into step beside him, smiling at the antics of barefooted children scampering agile as mountain goats in the direction of houses that had huge boulders built into their foundations; walls made of small stones and bricks fashioned out of mud from the river bed, then baked hard in the sun.

The schoolhouse, an exact replica of the rest of the village houses, had obviously once been a family home, she decided, and had her theory confirmed when she was ushered across the threshold into a huge ground-floor room.

'Only the first-floor rooms of village houses are

used by their inhabitants as living quarters—the largest one for sleeping in and another used as a kitchen-cum-sitting-room,' Stelios told her. 'Usually, the ground floor is also separated into two rooms, but, as you have no doubt guessed, the dividing wall in this house was removed when it was decided that it should be utilised as a schoolroom.'

'What is the purpose of those large earthenware jars?' She puzzled over three huge jars, bulbous around the middle and having sufficient space inside to provide a hiding place for half a dozen mischievous children.

'They're wine barrels. Even before the foundations of each house was laid a barrel had to be placed in the basement because, as they are so large, they could not be manoeuvred through doorways once the houses were built. Consequently, they cannot now be removed without either breaking them or pulling the house down. Grapes are placed in the barrels and trodden in the traditional way to produce wine juice. Some villager go further, and with the aid of stills produce a spirit known as *zivania*—an extremely potent brew that cannot be bought, but which you may be fortunate enough to be offered when invited into the homes of villagers whose hospitality is as warm and generous as their hearts.'

He had barely finished speaking when the first set of parents arrived—the village grocer and his wife who was carrying a basin which she shyly pressed into Petra's hands.

'*Beccaficos,* nicely boiled and sprinkled with

lemon juice,' she explained. 'Before eating them, *thespinis,* you must cut them open and extract a tiny hard ball which is their stomach and which is not edible. Then eat the whole bird as it is, preferably with some fresh bread and a glass of wine.'

Petra's sensitive stomach turned over, but somehow she managed to thank the woman for the basinful of tiny pickled birds that the islanders regarded as a great delicacy.

A flood of parents followed, all carrying gifts. Homemade cream cheese from the shepherd; a tin of black olives swimming in vinegar and oil from a farmer; an *oke* of fresh tomatoes from the greengrocer; a bunch of grapes from a courtyard vine; a still-warm unplucked chicken from the butcher; a silvery blue, rather plump fish with a black band around its tail which the fishmonger emphasised was 'for grilling only'; together with countless offerings of fruit, bottles of local wine, vegetables, freshly baked biscuits, preserves, and bunches of flowers picked by the children as welcoming gifts for their new teacher.

By the time the schoolroom had become filled with friendly, smiling faces, and a table was overflowing with expressions of gratitude extended by parents to the teacher whom the *kyrios* had managed to entice into their isolated village in order to instruct their children, Petra had been moved almost to tears, overwhelmed by kindness and generosity.

'*Efharisto!*' Thank you very much ...' she eventually stammered for the very last time. 'But there really was no need ...!'

'To each saint his candle, *thespinis*.' The broadly smiling butcher had evidently been elected spokesman. 'Every one of our children nurtures an ambition to speak fluent English, but up until your arrival it had not been found possible to provide them with a *frontistiria* in which to receive special instruction in subjects that they find especially difficult. In spite of a six-day-a-week attendance at school and three, sometimes four and five hours of homework each night, they are keen to learn more about their most popular subject. They could barely contain their excitement when they were informed of your imminent arrival.'

'But if they study so hard and for such long hours without a break, surely they should be allowed to take full advantage of their annual holidays!' she protested.

The butcher shrugged. 'It is all part of gaining an education in our sweet land. Students must work hard to prepare themselves for the very difficult university entrance exams.'

Petra's only regret, as they set off on the return journey home, was that the many invitations to stay to lunch had been declined by Stelios Heracles, whose pressure-of-work excuse had been received sympathetically by the hard working villagers. Even friendly shouts of, *'Kopiaste'*— 'come sit with me and share my meal'—from farmworkers sitting near the roadside spreading frugal meals of bread, cheese, olives and tomatoes on brightly checked napkins, received scant acknowledgement from the man brooding silently behind the wheel, his brow furrowed as if his mind was wrestling with some difficult, entirely absorbing problem.

They had passed through the huge bronze gates guarding the castle drive before she managed to find sufficient courage to intrude into his thoughts.

'Er . . . about my brother Gavin?'

'What?' His startled head swung towards her, almost as if, she decided resentfully, he had just become aware of her presence. 'I beg your pardon, would you mind repeating that statement?'

'My brother Gavin', she stressed desperately. 'I must know what's happening to him, whether he is to be released or . . . or . . .' she gulped, hardly daring to dwell upon the horrifying possibility, 'whether he is to be charged and sent for trial.'

With increased agitation she waited for his reply. He took his time, slowing the car to a crawl to negotiate a bend in the driveway before braking outside the entrance to the castle. Silently he helped her to alight, then roved brooding eyes over her pinched, anxious face before seemingly reaching some decision.

'May I leave you to amuse yourself for the rest of today, Miss Morrison? Depending upon the outcome of a number of important telephone calls, it is just possible that I may be in a position to offer a solution to the problem of your brother's future when you join me for dinner this evening.'

CHAPTER FIVE

AFTER doing scant justice to a light lunch of salad and fish Petra wandered upstairs to her bedroom feeling restless, her thoughts an emotional stew of hope and doubt, faith, and despair of even the influential Stelios Heracles managing to extricate Gavin from the clutches of aggressive Greek policemen.

For almost half an hour she sat gazing out of the window, seeing nothing, then when her own fearful, agitated company became unbearable she jumped to her feet, determined to seek out human contact rather than endure further hours of fraught solitude.

Her footsteps echoed eerily when she stepped into the brooding silence of the great hall. Nervously, keeping her eyes averted from the sightless visors of suits of armour with mailed fists clenched around a fearsome assortment of weapons, she headed towards a door she hoped might lead into a kitchen filled with friendly, chattering servants. But the large whitewashed room she discovered at the end of a passageway was deserted, its iron range bare, tables cleared, heavy black cooking pots hung neatly around the walls. The scent of geraniums wafted from pots placed so that their fragrance could be carried on the breeze drifting through a half open window, but there was no welcoming aroma of coffee, no cheerful voice to greet her as she wandered forlornly around the deserted kitchen.

Siesta time. *Of course!* Belatedly, she remembered the ritual of shops closing down shutters; streets emptying, fields and vineyards left baking in solitude for as long as it took the sun to shed the worst of its noonday heat.

She half turned on her heel, about to retreat to her room, when the rattling of tin and a faint smell of paraffin attracted her attention. Curiously she walked across to a door giving outside access, then hurried to assist when she saw Sophia struggling to lift a large tin can.

'Let me help you with that, Sophia!'

The surprised old servant straightened, almost dropping the can on to her toes.

'Indeed you must not, *thespinis!*' she disapproved. 'The smell of paraffin clings to hands and clothes even after thorough washing. I would not wish the *kyrios* to be angered by the knowledge that his guest had been allowed to carry out the duties of a servant.'

'Then he should ensure that there is a man ready to be called upon to help you with messy jobs and heavy lifting!' Petra countered, her tone sharp with annoyance at the way Greek males were apt to turn a blind eye upon degrading tasks carried out by their womenfolk while at the same time taking care to ensure that their donkeys were never overladen.

Sophia threw back her head with a gesture of scorn, her dark eyes rolling. 'Preparing charcoal is far too exacting an art to be left to men,' she snorted. 'The whole business is a ritual that has to be taken seriously if meat is to be grilled to perfection! But you must excuse me, *thespinis*, for neglecting my duties,' hurriedly she wiped her hands on her apron. 'If you will give me a few minutes to wash my hands I'll attend to whichever request has brought you in search of a servant. Really, you should not be here, if there is anything you need all you have to do is ring . . .'

'All I need is company, Sophia.' Firmly, Petra hooked a hand under the handle of the can and removed its weight from Sophia's gnarled fingers. 'Finish what you're doing, if you must, then afterwards perhaps you and I could share a pot of coffee?'

An anticipatory gleam brightened Sophia's eyes, acting upon Petra's instincts like a warning signal. Too late, she remembered the old woman's tendency towards matchmaking, her intense curiosity about the guest she had obviously decided would make an ideal wife for her beloved employer.

Teasing remarks, made specifically by her father to arouse the indignation of her passionately Greek mother, echoed from the past to bring a pensive smile to her lips. 'If ever you should be unfortunate enough to become engaged to a Greek, you will find yourself being subjected to intense suspicion, an interrogation of your background which will be held by everyone of about two thousand members of your fiancé's family!' he had grinned. 'You will be poked and prodded, vetted and inquisitioned until the fears of every single one of them have been allayed. Marriage to a Greek means taking on not only a partner, but also an entire family of in-laws who will continue to view you with suspicion until the birth of your first child, at least!'

Sophia's voice intruded. 'I would enjoy that very much, *thespinis.*' Eagerly she resumed her task of igniting paraffin-soaked charcoal piled in the middle of a metal trough by tossing a lighted match as close as possible to the highly inflammable fuel. Then immediately it flared, she placed a chimney made out of a large tin can with both ends removed on top of the crackling charcoal and began fanning the flames with a piece of stiff cardboard until the roaring died down, the smoke had dispersed, and a few well aimed stabs with a poker produced a uniform layer of smouldering charcoal over the base of the trough.

'There, that will do nicely!' Flushed with heat and exertion, Sophia straightened, well satisfied with the results of her labours. 'I will leave it now to digest until it is time to begin grilling kebabs for dinner.'

With the air of a hostess anxious to extend hospitality to an unexpected guest, she then ushered Petra into the kitchen and insisted that she remained seated at a scrubbed-white wooden table while she bustled around the kitchen setting out cups and a plateful of honey cakes as she waited for water in an *imbrika* to boil.

Amused by her air of great expectancy, Petra sat silently watching the brewing ritual, and was unprepared for the offensive that was launched even before the dregs of thick, sweet coffee had had time to settle.

'Because I was never in a position to marry,'

Sophia confided, 'the *kyrios* is as dear to me as the son I never had.' Puzzling spots of colour appeared high in her cheeks as she continued abruptly: 'And as he, too, has always treated me more as a member of his family than as a servant, I feel entitled to worry about his future happiness— hope that I will see him married with a family of infants before I go to the little cypress trees.'

Petra frowned, recognising an expression her grandfather had occasionally used when referring to the chilling eventuality of death. Tall, ancient trees named after the island upon which they had once been worshipped were planted in borders around churches and cemeteries, towering green and stately long after the stone they were meant to protect had begun to crumble, thriving, thrusting symbols of life after death.

Aware of the superstitious melancholy veining the character of the islanders, Petra attempted to lighten the conversation by sidetracking gently:

'Why were you unable to marry, Sophia?'

'Because our dowry system demands that a girl must supply a house in exchange for a new name and a wedding ring,' the woman admitted simply. 'During my teens, all leisure hours were spent embroidering tableclothes, pillowcases, and doilies with intricate needlework, slowly counting stitch after stitch, taking weeks, often months, to complete items intended to provide proof of skill and industry to a prospective husband. But,' she shrugged, her lined face wrinkling into an expression of regret, 'after seven years of storing items into an overflowing chest, I was forced to acknowledge that my role in life was that of a permanent spinster. Girls without property are at a disadvantage in the marriage market. No house—no husband!'

Suddenly she leant across the table, her pensive look displaced by a hard, compelling stare.

'Which brings me back to the subject I was about to raise. Do you possess a dowry, *thespinis*—some exchangeable asset that might tempt a handsome, eligible bachelor to contemplate matrimony?'

Petra's cheeks flamed. A rebuke sprang to her lips, an angry indictment of the persistent old matchmaker whose remarks had reduced her to the level of a piece of livestock being sized up and haggled over in some cattle market. Even though she recognised anxiety in Sophia's eyes, a hint of misgiving betrayed by skin wrinkling around lips pursed with uncertainty, she found herself scolding coldly:

'Mercifully, circumstances have changed dramatically since your young days, Sophia! Marriage no longer means a contractual exchange of goods and legal relationships, but is a mutual declaration of love, a public vow made by lovers to become as one, to help one another through adversity, to be sympathetic to each other's ailments, to share happiness in health, to instil into their children the same high ideals and unmercenary code of behaviour followed by themselves! The very idea of marital status being exchanged for property is abhorrent to me!' she concluded with the vehemence of a scholar whose only equivalent to a bottom drawer was a wall lined with framed diplomas and a briefcase overflowing with glowing testimonials.

'I have offended you, *thespinis!* I am so sorry, I did not intend . . .' Sophia's voice trembled into silence as she stared across the table at the suddenly animated girl upon whom anger had reacted in the manner of a kiss upon the lips of a sleeping beauty.

All the worry and strain caused by Gavin's arrest, all the guilt she felt about the lies she had been forced to tell, all the fear and unease imposed upon her by the dark, brooding looks and cryptic remarks passed by the man used to living in the shadow of Olympus, the mythical residence of ancient Greek gods that was off limits to all mortals, was contained in the glare Petra directed towards the worried old servant. But when she saw Sophia cower, her anger evaporated. Ashamed of her uncharacteristic burst of anger, she strove to make amends by forcing brightness into her tone as she urged.

'Oh, let's change the subject, Sophia!' She cast around in her mind for some thought to lighten Sophia's burden of misery, then seized upon a glimmer of inspiration. 'I've had an idea! How would you like to read my fortune?'

As if by magic Sophia's face brightened. 'If that is your wish, *thespinis!'*

'It is.' Feeling greatly relieved, Petra pushed her empty coffee cup across the table.

'No, no!' Smiling broadly, Sophia pushed it back towards her. 'To have your fortune told you must turn your coffee cup upside down. Put the saucer over the top of the cup, then swiftly turn both cup and saucer over. That's it! The cup must be completely drained, so you must tilt it on to the side of the saucer and let it stand for a while.'

But when Petra attempted to follow her instructions the cup held fast, apparently reluctant to part company with the saucer.

'Good! Good . . .!' Sophia clapped, obviously overwhelmed with excitement. 'When the cup sticks to the saucer it is a sign that the lover you desire is in love with you!'

When Petra tugged hard and handed her the cup she finally managed to dislodge from the saucer, Sophia drooled almost reverently over the remaining maze of thick sediment.

'I see church bells,' she intoned, 'almost at the rim of the cup—which means that a wedding is imminent!'

Petra suppressed an impatient sigh at this further evidence of Sophia's one-track mind. Yet in spite of her scepticism, her heart sank when she saw the old woman frown.

'There is a trail of bitterness leading straight to the door of the church.' Vigorously she shook the cup as if trying to dislodge the unwelcome omen, then continued peering intently. 'Ah, but there is sweetness to be found, *elika,* if you are prepared to sift the dregs in search of it! See for yourself!' She turned the cup to enable Petra to follow the direction of her pointing finger. 'Can you make out a halo of shining Greek gold encircling the fierce-looking profile of a man with a lionesque mane of hair?'

To have lingered another minute would have meant having to inflict upon the stubborn old woman a further scolding. So in a bid to avoid hurting her feelings, Petra jumped to her feet and made towards the door, casting across her shoulder a look designed to project tolerant amusement.

'Thank you, Sophia, but I think I've heard enough! I suspect it may be wrong to attempt to pry into the future. The chain of destiny is too heavy to allow frail mortals such as myself to handle more than one link at a time!'

Feeling even less inclined towards solitude now that Sophia had managed to unsettle her further, Petra almost ran across the great hall of antiquity to strain open one half of the heavy double doors that had withstood centuries of assault upon the castle fortress. Intending to take a stroll, she tripped down the flight of stone steps into an atmosphere that was pure magic, the unspoilt beauty of cypress-coated peaks; birds flitting among trees spreading a blanket of green around turrets and towers transformed by strong sunlight in the sort of setting that would not have looked out of place in a book of fairytales—a place where Prince Charmings on white chargers brought golden-haired princesses to live happily ever after...

Slowly she wandered down the drive, sniffing intoxicating mountain air laden with the scent of rosemary and thyme and a citrus tang rising from lemon and orange groves. At the end of the driveway she turned right on to the rough, winding road that led down to the village, then a few yards on she rounded a bend, to find the road completely blocked by a flock of meandering sheep.

Startled by her abrupt appearance, they scattered, their frantic baaing attracting the attention of an old shepherd who had momentarily deserted his flock in order to carry out the self-imposed duty of topping up the lamp of a wayside shrine with fresh olive oil. When he scrambled back on to the road to calm his flock with a few gruff grunts and an assortment of unintelligible noises she saw that he was wearing *vraka,* the traditional baggy trousers favoured by some of the older peasants, and a well-worn army surplus jacket worn over a thick-knit jumper to provide the warmth necessary before dawn when the sun's rays did not reach the mountain's higher pastures. A white kerchief twisted into a bandeau to protect his brow from the heat; craggy, weatherbeaten features; bushy eyebrows and moustache, and a rough, unshaven chin gave him the look of a fierce mountain tribesman. But his voice when he greeted her was low-pitched and courteous.

'*Yia sou, thespinis!*' he nodded, placing both hands on top of his shepherd's crook to lean, obviously delighted at the prospect of a pleasant chat breaking the monotony of his day.

'Hello,' she responded with equal enthusiasm. 'Your animals look healthy and well fed.' She smiled down at the sheep that had returned to surround the shepherd, jostling for position around his knees. 'But how overburdened with fleece on such a hot day!'

'Not for much longer, *thespinis,*' his teeth flashed white against nut brown skin. 'At this very moment shearers are waiting to deprive each shaggy animal of the *flokati* rug it is wearing on its

back! Sheep are wonderful creatures,' he boasted
fondly. 'We islanders could barely survive without
their milk that provides light, creamy butter,
yoghurt, and our famous *feta* cheese which you
must often have eaten with salad. As well as the
rugs that are so popular with tourists, their fleece
is spun into woollen yarn, and as for the meat
itself——!' he raised bunched fingertips to his lips
and threw a kiss to the four winds. 'Nothing tastes
more delicious than lamb slowly roasted over an
outdoor spit—especially the head, which is the
tastiest delicacy of all!'

In spite of sunrays basting through her blouse,
Petra shuddered as once more she came face to
face with the contradictory Greek nature that saw
nothing wrong in rearing an animal and then
eating its head; in falling in love with youth and
beauty and then choosing to marry a pile of
stones; in being kind and hospitable to strangers
and at the same time ruthlessly determined to
achieve personal aims.

'I must go,' she decided, clenching suddenly icy
fingers, 'the air is growing cooler.'

'The first cool breath of evening,' the shepherd
nodded, then, just as she was turning away, he
confirmed her previous misgivings by thrusting a
hand inside his jacket to ease a small wire cage
from its dark, stuffy resting place. 'I wonder,
thespinis, if you would care to give a home to this
orphaned canary?'

She stared with horror at the limp puff of yellow
feathers lying on the floor of the cage which a
thick coat and jumper had rendered an airless
tomb.

'Oh, the poor thing!' she choked. 'It looks half dead . . .!'

'It will soon recover,' he assured her. 'In any case, it would surely have suffered more had I not rescued it from being released into the wild where there is no hope of escape from winged predators. It was the pet of an old lady whose husband objected to its incessant singing. In the early hours of the morning it wakened him; in the afternoon it disturbed his siesta, and in the early evening when he tried to relax on his porch he found the bird's continuous trilling an aggravation. Take it, please, *thespinis!* I know you will treat it well—its name, by the way, is Pini.'

Clutching her precious burden to her breast, Petra ran back along the road, then panted up the driveway. In her haste to reach the kitchen to ask Sophia's advice she took a short cut through the grounds, then sped round the corner of the castle, cannoning straight into Stelios Heracles, who was striding from the direction of the stables.

'What the devil . . .!' His hands shot out to steady her as she rocked on her heels, winded by the unexpected collision. 'Are you all right?' he questioned sharply. 'What is that thing you are clutching like a talisman against all evil?'

'It's a bird,' she gulped, 'a canary that's dying from too much heat and a lack of air! I must try to revive it,' she wobbled, her wide eyes flooding with tears, 'but I'm not sure how . . .'

Swiftly, with a competence that earned him a tremulous smile of gratitude, he opened the door of the cage and cupped the still ball of feathers in the palm of his hand.

'That cage is far too small,' he snapped as she ran by his side attempting to keep pace with his striding progress towards the door leading into the kitchen.

'Fetch a small glass of water, someone!' he called out to a roomful of milling servants. Then, hooking a foot beneath a chair, he dragged it outside into the open air and sat down, massaging the bird's breast with a finger as he lifted it up to his mouth and began blowing steady, gentle breaths of air into its gaping beak.

Unaware that silent sobs were shuddering through her body, Petra leant across his shoulder, willing the small, limp head to move; a wing to lift, a heartbeat to disturb the still roundness of the feathered body. Servant crowded at a distance, shaking their heads to communicate doubt about the success of the life-saving operation, but Stelios continued with infinite patience massaging and breathing until long after Petra had given up hope.

She sighed with regret, and was just about to suggest that he should abandon the exercise so that the tiny creature could be laid to rest, when an almost imperceptible movement of its feathered breast drew her startled attention.

'Stelios,' she breathed against his ear, completely oblivious to the fact that she had used such a familiar form of address, 'I think I saw a sign of movement! I'm sure I did. Look, there's another! And another ... *Stelios,* you've done it, the bird's alive!'

Success was confirmed when a pair of gem-bright eyes flickered open and one panicking wing lifted as the canary attempted a feeble escape from the hands that had saved its life.

Ecstatic with relief, Petra flung an arm as far as she could reach across the width of Stelios's broad shoulders and bent her head close to his to peer like a proud mother upon an alert, bravely struggling offspring.

'Fetch a glass of water!' Stelios called out, his cheek brushing against hers as he tossed a questing glance across his shoulder. 'Also, we need a cage. Sophia, do you know whether or not we have a birdcage on the premises?'

The servants surged forward, delighted to see smiles radiating from the face of the young English girl who for several anxious minutes had seemed ready to burst into tears.

'I have a spare cage at home, *thespinis!*' a voice offered.

'And so have I! My children's pet died only last week; I feel I should wait a short while before suggesting a replacement!'

'Certainly we have a birdcage!' Sophia elbowed her way forward. 'Is there a home on the island which has not, at some time or another, satisfied the needs of its children by choosing a canary as a pet in preference to a destructive cat or a dog that requires much feeding?' Imperiously, she called out to one of the younger servants.

'Nikos! Go down to the cellar and bring up the cage you will find under a dustsheet in a far corner. Hurry now!' Already the bird is getting stronger—look how eager it is to quench its thirst!'

Less than five minutes later Nikos returned triumphant bearing a large ornately gilded cage, and the servants dispersed amid much goodhumoured badinage to continue with their duties.

With a sigh of complete contentment Petra clipped back the door of the cage, inviting Stelios to scoop the bird inside what was, in comparison with its previous residence, a palace fit for a feathered king. But instead of releasing the nervously pulsating bird immediately, he cupped his palms into a detaining cell and regarded his prisoner thoughtfully.

'It is not often,' he mused, 'that one is able to study at close quarters the intimate habits and behaviour of a shy, timid creature, consoled by the certainty that however hard it may struggle it cannot get away.'

Petra's blood ran cold. His gaze was fixed upon the tiny yellow bird whose panic was increasing second by second as it fought against the pressure of alien fingers, yet instinct warned her that his words were directed towards herself, that his gentle persecution of the creature that owed him its life contained a message too frightening for her to contemplate.

'A flower seen for the first time can be picked and examined at leisure,' he continued tormenting, 'but often a bird is observed for mere seconds before it runs for cover or flies out of reach of its admirer.'

She gave a nervous jump when suddenly he released the bird and snapped shut the door of the cage.

'Catching ends the pleasure of the chase.' His voice held a savage edge. 'Obviously, that must be the reason why men quickly become indifferent to wives who always rush to greet them instead of occasionally running the other way.'

CHAPTER SIX

WHEN a Greek is upset he sounds furious. Absently, Petra brushed the palm of her hand over the tiny leaves of a basil plant, then stooped to inhale the scent that freshened the air inside her bedroom like a spray wafting a delicate, mint-scented perfume. She had dressed for dinner with special care, choosing to wear her only decent dress—a sleeveless sheath made of whisper-soft silk which Gavin had once been moved to observe matched exactly the grey-blue veil that shimmered over her eyes whenever she was moved to the brink of tears. She lingered by the window, trembling at the prospect of having to endure the company of the man whose rasped words had communicated resentment of a duty to wed which he obviously regarded as a threat to his freedom, a man whose calculating eyes, intimidating physique and dominating will made her feel nervous, insignificant, and frighteningly vulnerable.

If only Gavin were here! she fretted, badly in need of a confidant, missing her brother's lighthearted teasing, his cheerful grin, the optimism she grasped like a lifeline whenever she was depressed. But Gavin was imprisoned—she winced from the shocking reminder—not trilling blissfully like Pini who was fluttering and hopping around his spacious gilt cage, but probably sitting lonely and dejected in a dark, cold cell, willing her, *relying* on her, to get him out!

The thought acted like the spur she needed to snatch up a light woollen stole and hurry downstairs, determined to confront the man of authority who was powerful enough to control Gavin's destiny merely by lifting a finger to dial a number on the telephone.

But her wave of courage ebbed immediately she caught sight of her suave, impeccably dressed host waiting at the foot of the marble staircase. Ancient Moorish oil-lamps suspended on chains from a ceiling lost among evening shadows guttered in the path of draughts penetrating crumbling masonry and age-shrunken windows and doors, turning the hall into a Danteesque inferno of flickering flame and dense voids of darkness.

'Kalispera, elika!'

In spite of an ultra-civilised effect achieved with the aid of a perfectly tailored dinner jacket, sharply creased trousers, and a crisply elegant evening shirt displaying a glint of gold links at each cuff, Stelios Heracles looked perfectly at home in his satanic environment.

'Would you care for a drink before dinner?' He eased a hand under her elbow to lead her across the hall.

'No, thank you,' she refused primly, nervous of a dark Greek presence whose bold eyes and aquiline features betrayed some far-off strain of Moorish blood. 'I don't care for the taste of alcohol.'

He laughed softly as he guided her inside a room whose walls, lined with pleated silk the colour of buttermilk, imposed upon her a strong impression that she was being led inside a Bedouin tent.

'I'm beginning to understand how you earned your unwelcome title, Miss Grundy!' he glinted wickedly. 'Quite unintentionally, I feel sure, you managed to refuse the offer of a drink as if you had just been invited to indulge in an act of debauchery. Certainly, the sexual associations in names given to some of our local drinks are very noticeable—Maiden's Tears; Volcanic Virgin, and Bachelor's Bracer, to quote just a few examples— nevertheless, all I am offering at this precise moment,' he mocked, strolling across to a drinks cabinet, 'is an innocuous rose cordial, a drink distilled from the flower chosen by your country as its national emblem because of its symbolic connection with females who are paragons of virtue. Sweet and fragrant,' he drawled, bending to hand her a pink drink in a tall frosted glass, 'but with a slow-to-melt heart of crushed ice!'

With cheeks flaming pink as the glass that was freezing her fingers, Petra sat with eyes downcast, wondering how to cope with the devil in a tormenting mood, how to avoid further embarrassing conversation by introducing the topic uppermost in her mind.

Stelios sat down opposite with a glass of wine and unwittingly provided the opening she needed with the casual enquiry:

'How is your rescued pet? No doubt you have already begun smothering it into a state of lethargy, stifling all initiative to fend alone, just as you did your brother!'

'Pini seems well on the way to recovery,' she told him stiffly, steeling herself to remain calm, to continue placidly sipping her drink before beginning a mildly accusing barrage. 'But then one can never gauge with certainty the feelings of any creature confined behind bars. Gavin, for instance, must have made a tremendous effort to sound as composed as he did during the one telephone call he has been allowed to make since his arrest.' Forgetting her earlier resolution, she leant forward to plead: 'This morning, Minister, you intimated that you might have some news of my brother later in the day.' She paused to swallow the lump of trepidation that had suddenly blocked her throat, then raced her remaining words in case her voice should break. 'Please don't keep me in suspense—whether the news is good or bad, for heaven's sake tell me now!'

She sensed from the unhurried way he laid down his glass before rising to stretch to his full height that he had every intention of keeping her on tenterhooks.

'Such a weighty discussion must be postponed until after we've eaten. We Greeks, irrespective of status, regard eating as one of the greatest joys in life. Much thought goes into the preparation and serving of our food, so in fairness to Sophia and her helpers, we must attach the same degree of importance to our meal as did one ancient Persian culinary wizard who divided pleasure into six categories—food, drink, clothes, sex, scent and sound—then selected food as the noblest and most consequential pleasure of all.'

'But, Minister . . .!' She jumped to her feet to protest but was coolly interrupted.

'Mere hours ago you called me Stelios! Please continue to do so, and in return I promise that never again, unless deliberately provoked, shall I cast a cloud of hurt over your beautiful eyes by referring to you as Miss Grundy!'

In sober silence she accompanied him into the dining-room, then faltered just inside the threshold to stare, intimidated by the opulence of a spacious, gilded interior bathed in the golden glow of light cast by an ornate chandelier suspended over a long, narrow table glistening with silver dishes and cutlery; crystal wine glasses and tall slender-necked water jugs; crisp white napkins and a centrepiece of flowers spiking the air with the heady scent of wild violets, pale lilies, and coyly drooping heads of columbine. Tall windows draped in rich velvet spilled a flow of deep burgundy red the length of panelled walls inset at regular intervals with strips of mirror reflecting her awed approach within each gilded frame.

Nervously, she murmured her thanks to the formally attired manservant who assisted her into a high-backed brocaded chair, then failed dismally to respond to the amused smile cast by the man enthroned with godlike superiority at the head of the superbly appointed table.

Conscious of his intent scrutiny, she mustered all the confidence she had gained while helping Lady Holland to extend hospitality to foreign ambassadors, and strove to appear at ease when she indicated to a hovering manservant her choice of titbits from a bewildering selection of *mézé*, dishes of delicious-looking hors d'oeuvres made appealing to the eye as well as to the appetite by artistic attention applied to displaying pale green cucumbers next to a creamy dip; cubes of hard white cheese with bright red tomatoes; deep purple figs with pink *taramasalata*; yellow and white garnishes of hardboiled eggs, lemon wedges, red radishes, and deep green, delicately flavoured sprinklings of chopped parsley.

'I'm pleased to see that you appreciate the need for small helpings of our traditional Cypriot starter, *elika*.' His dark eyes derided the minute amount of food on her plate. '*Mézés* means delicacy, and delicacies, in common with members of your own delicate sex, are always more appreciated if sampled in small doses.'

'That remark betrays an extremely sexist outlook,' she returned steadily. 'You're surely not implying that eating and drinking are pleasures appreciated only by men?'

The clash of dark eyes meeting blue over a bowl of riotous blossoms was almost audible.

'Not entirely,' he drawled, obviously intrigued by her flash of spirit, 'but in common with most of my countrymen I do believe that it is a woman's duty to ensure that plates are kept full and her husband kept happy. Regrettably, even in this mountain stronghold some old customs treasured by men are being allowed to fade.'

Petra eyed him warily, suspecting that the napkin he had lifted to his lips was screening a smile.

'In days gone by,' he continued smoothly, 'wives served meals to husbands reclining upon a carpeted floor supported by huge feather cushions while they dipped their fingers into platters placed upon a low table, washing their hands in bowls of rosewater replenished at regular intervals by their devoted wives.'

'Slaves would be a more apt description!' she flared, incensed by a masculine conceit which she had long ago decided was a vice inherent in all undeniably attractive men; shaken by the return of the puzzling sensation she had experienced while he had been ministering to Pini—when his cheek had brushed against hers for a cool, intimate second and her heart had reacted as if suddenly possessed of fluttering, panic-stricken wings.

'Perhaps so,' he agreed, his features hardening into a mask of scowling ill humour, 'but the curse of slavery is shared equally between the sexes. No man alive can boast absolute freedom, each one is forced either by conscience or convention to conform.'

A substantial dish of *moussaka* with a minced meat filling and a crust of toasted cheese was followed by skewered cubes of chicken and lamb grilled over charcoal. Desultorily, Petra picked over each item of food on her plate, making a pretence of eating before pushing her plate aside. But the sight of a platter laden with sweetmeats— still-warm puffs of pastry sprinkled with icing sugar and dripping with honey—forced her to voice a protest.

'I'm sorry!' When a manservant approached with the platter she waved him away. 'I simply couldn't eat another bite.'

'You have the appetite of a canary,' Stelios observed unkindly, nevertheless he followed her example by waving the sweet away. 'We'll have our drinks in the blue drawing-room where it is much more comfortable,' he declared, tossing aside his napkin as he rose to push his chair away from the table.

'Nothing more for me, thank you.' She shied in panic from the proposed intimacy of being enclosed within a dark blue den of seduction with only a moody, unpredictable devil for company. 'I still haven't finished my cordial.'

'I was not suggesting that you should pour infinite quantities of alcohol down your throat,' he growled sarcastically. 'We Cypriots look upon drink as an aid to making new friendships. A few sips of wine helps to loosen the tongue, enabling shy individuals to relax and unhappy ones to view the future with optimism. After all, as you have no pressing engagement looming, what possible objection can you have to sharing with me what might turn out to be a very enlightening evening?'

He had issued no command, yet when he stood aside waiting for her to precede him out of the room, she knew that he was expecting an obedient reaction. Her lashes swept down to hide a glint of rebellion, yet she did as he expected, knowing that she had no choice but to pander to the whims of the Greek despot who possessed the influence needed to free her brother, whose ego had to be flattered, whose massive conceit would have to be quietly, subtly manipulated if ever she were to achieve her aim.

The blue drawing-room must have been the smallest room in the castle, even so, it seemed to Petra more spacious than the entire interior of her flat. Comfortable divans and armchairs had been

arranged to form an oasis of cream brocaded
comfort that helped lighten the density of walls
and curtains matching the deep blue depth of her
companion's mood. Torch-shaped lamps blazed at
intervals around the walls, but their glow barely
encroached upon the sumptuous divan which she
tried to avoid, only to be cleverly outmanoeuvred
by a hand that grasped her shoulder, checking her
instinctive retreat and levering her downwards
until she felt in danger of being swamped by a
cocoon of plush upholstery and piles of silken
cushions.

'Let me get you a drink that will help to relax
your tension,' he offered dryly. 'At this moment,
you remind me of a stiffly-perched bird which I
may be required to stalk with patience and
cunning if ever I am to get within range!'

He left her to blush unseen while he turned his
attention upon a manservant who had just
arrived pushing a trolley laden with an assortment
of bottles, a tray of pretzels, and the inevitable
small dishes of peanuts to which all Cypriot males
seemed madly addicted.

'Thank you, Thasos,' he nodded dismissal, 'I
will pour out the drinks myself. Please ensure that
we are left undisturbed for the rest of the evening.'

'Very well, *kyrie*.' The servant's response was
bland, yet instinctively Petra stiffened, her finely
attuned ear sensitive to a nuance of satisfaction so
faint that anyone less familiar than herself with
Greek tone and temperament would have found it
impossible to interpret. A feeling that she was
being manipulated, made to play a part in a scene
set up so many times before that even servants had

become familiar with it, sent prickles of alarm chasing along her spine.

Why hadn't she foreseen the danger threatening any female, however lacking in sexual experience, foolish enough to condone solitude with a Greek whose athletic namesake had been worshipped as the god of physical prowess!

'A small glass of *filfar* should help to educate your unsophisticated palate!' She came back to earth with a start, her eyes unable for a second to focus upon the glass he was holding out towards her. 'You'll find it a perfect after-dinner drink, an orange-flavoured liqueur whose origins have been lost in time. The drink itself would almost certainly have vanished had not the son of a family owning extensive orange groves discovered an old recipe which an ancestor of his had been given by monks who once lived in a monastery that today is no more than a ruined shell. Fortunately, the finder of the forgotten recipe recalled from childhood the method used by his mother and grandmother to make the liqueur. He began experimenting, confining the results of his labours to his own family at first, then eventually giving away bottles to friends whose clamouring for more convinced him that his product should be marketed. Try a little,' he urged, 'and tell me what you think.'

Petra gripped the stem of the glass between nervous fingers, confounded by the stroke of his warm breath against her brow, startled by his swift fluidity of movement when he swooped to sit down beside her, close enough to offer one broad shoulder as a backrest. Mesmerised by dark eyes glinting a command to drink, she lifted the glass to her lips and gulped down half its contents, then gasped when the spirit began blazing a fiery orange trail down her throat, then throughout her entire body, reaching every curled-up toe and tingling fingertip.

Hastily she set down the glass, eyeing it with the distaste she would have shown some shocking ritual vessel. But damage had already been imposed upon her senses by liqueur that blended the taste of bitter oranges with the sweetness of honey.

'Potent drinks should always be sipped,' Stelios protested on a note of laughter. 'Because of the speed with which you disposed of that, *elika*, I suspect that you will shortly be feeling as if you have been given the wings necessary to fly out of your cloister!'

'You should have warned me!' she coughed, then swallowed hard, trying to rid her throat of the molten liqueur.

'I do wish to warn you. Or perhaps caution would be a better choice of word.' The plethora of moods that had plagued him all evening—a gamut ranging from light amusement to deep cynicism that had led her to wonder whether it was possible for a man elected to lead; for a man used to making and acting upon instant decisions, to be troubled by uncertainty—seemed to have settled upon a final choice of grim resignation.

'You squander so much of your love and devotion, *elika*, it would not be fair of me to offer you a choice of action without stressing the need for a cautious answer. But then,' he smiled thinly, 'perhaps such a dedicated martyr as yourself will consider that she has been given no choice at all! Though our acquaintanceship is of such short duration, I am convinced that you are likely to agree with the meekness of a lamb to being sacrificed on the altar of sisterly love.'

Her fearful eyes fastened upon his sombre features, but she remained still and silent, chilled by a certainty that he was leading up to some ultimatum concerning Gavin. She waited, mentally urging him to continue, anxious for the situation to be clarified even though she nurtured no hope of compassion from the horned god in situ. But although he must have sensed her agony of mind, he took time to pick a peanut from a dish and crunch it to extinction between his teeth before subjecting her to further verbal prowling.

'Here in Cyprus, there have been many occasions in the past when young men caught breaking the law have opted for "instant justice"—that is, to stand trial by a jury made up of local villagers rather than risk the penalties handed out by an authorised court of law. Usually, the culprits were punished by village chiefs ordering each offender to work for so many weeks in the fields—or months, according to the seriousness of the crime. That way, honour was satisfied all round and the young man's family was saved the ordeal of having shame publicly branded upon its name.'

Petra relaxed, resisting an urge to sag with relief when his meaning became clear. A ghost of a smile drifted around her mouth as inwardly she scolded an over-active imagination that had led her to suspect the presence of some bizarre motive behind his carefully chosen words.

'Are you telling me in a roundabout way that you've decided to submit Gavin to a court of instant justice?' Starry-eyed, she relaxed against cushions clustered into a brilliant halo around her pale features. 'Why didn't you come straight to the point,' she laughed shakily, 'instead of meandering around the subject as if you considered such an idea unacceptable? I think it's a perfect solution,' she sparkled. 'Gavin is certain to consider tackling tasks around the village infinitely preferable to languishing in prison for an indefinite period!'

She leant forward to urge: 'How soon can he be released? Tomorrow? The day after, perhaps . . .?'

'Perhaps.' Much to her surprise she saw no change in his grim demeanour. If anything, his jawline looked even tighter, his expression a shade more austere. 'The date of your brother's release is dependent upon the time taken by ourselves to reach an agreement,' he told her, holding her eyes on a direct course. 'After a great deal of argument, I have managed to persuade the police to release your brother into my custody and to leave charges against him in abeyance pending my report, which is to be made at my own discretion, regarding his attitude towards authority and his behaviour in general. If my report should turn out to be favourable, then all charges will be permanently dropped and your brother will be free to leave Cyprus without a stain on his character. If, however, he should not turn out to be as responsible and incorruptible as you claim, then I shall not hesitate to hand him back to the police with a recommendation that criminal proceedings should be allowed to run their normal course. I need hardly point out,' he concluded grimly, 'that such a recommendation would almost certainly be regarded as an indictment of instability.'

'But that's wonderful!' Petra cried out in delight, confident that Gavin would be prepared to co-operate with the first stipulation, thereby cancelling out the last. 'Oh, *Minister*—Stelios. . . .!' she amended with an embarrassed blush, 'I can't tell you how grateful I am, how happy you've made me . . .' she faltered, beaming appreciation with eyes of liquid blue. But when his eyes remained guarded and his mouth took on a sharp sabre's edge she felt a stirring of misgiving.

'There's just one more condition which requires careful consideration,' he clamped, chilling her slender frame into alert stillness. 'In an effort to talk the police authorities around to my way of thinking, I was forced to make a rather drastic statement . . .'

She offered no resistance when he reached out to cup her tightly clenched hands between his palms. 'I need a wife, *elika*,' his voice lowered to a soft, persuasive murmur that turned her bones to water. 'For too long I have turned a deaf ear to the voice of conscience urging me to settle down, to accept the bondage of domesticity and all its attendant drawbacks in order to ensure the continuity of my family name. The choice of marriage in . exchange for a son is what I'm offering, sweet Petra! A marriage that calls for little sacrifice from a girl who lacks money, who is badly in need of a protector and a home filled with children of her own.'

She was too shocked to respond other than with a wide-eyed stare teeming with emotions she was incapable of putting into words—an entreaty to confess that some satyr of cruel humour had prompted him to make her the butt of an illogical joke; a plea for his assurance that there had been no steely threat linking his chain of words.

She shuddered from his touch when lightly he stroked an encouraging hand across her cheek before tipping up her chin with a forceful finger.

'I cannot reward your honest virtue with deceit,' he murmured throatily, unaware that his words were grating upon her tender conscience. 'At the moment, there is no special woman in my life—but tomorrow,' he shrugged, 'next week, or next month, there almost certainly will be.'

Surprisingly, the casual admission jarred out of her a breathless protest. 'Then why don't you marry one of your attractive harem?'

'Because I subscribe to the doctrine of men of the East who maintain that one woman can never be enough, that it is a man's right to be able to choose his companion according to his mood.'

Petra hissed in an angry breath, then before spirit had time to desert her condemned his audacity.

'I love my brother dearly. Yet even though love is said to have drawn women towards many things—towards violence, towards madness, even towards death—it will never be allowed to draw me into such a disastrous marriage!'

He recoiled sharply, obviously amazed by her shocking ingratitude.

'If that is how you view the prospect of marriage

to me then obviously we need waste no further time in discussion.' He stood up, drawing himself tall with enormous dignity. 'Unfortunately for your brother, I now feel you have left me no option but to inform the police that they must deal with him as they see fit, now that the cancellation of our wedding has rid me of any obligation to accept responsibility for the actions of a reckless, foolhardy, totally irresponsible brother-in-law!'

CHAPTER SEVEN

'*GAVIN!*' Petra almost stumbled down the steps of the castle in her haste to reach her wan-faced, shaken-looking brother who was easing himself out of the passenger seat of Stelios's car. 'How are you?' She hugged him, laughing and crying at the same time. 'Did they treat you all right? *Darling*, you've lost weight . . .!'

All the heartache and worry of the past few days faded into insignificance as her eyes devoured his pale features, and his rakish young frame trembled within the circle of her arms.

'I've not yet recovered from the shock of being released into the custody of my future *brother-in-law*!' He slewed a glance that was far from friendly towards Stelios who was standing a few yards away, regarding their rapturous reunion with a look of amused tolerance. 'It simply isn't your style to act on impulse, Petra,' he condemned in a low-pitched mutter. 'You've been on the island less than a couple of weeks, yet I've just been informed that tomorrow you intend marrying that damned arrogant Greek!'

Her heart sank at the note of petulance in his tone. Gavin had always adopted an aggrieved stance whenever any of her actions had displeased him. Obviously, he was far from overjoyed at the prospect of having to share her affections with any other man—and especially not with a husband who would be entitled to first call upon her loyalty. Though every instinct was urging her to assure him that he had not been relegated to second place in her affections, that far from being in love with her, Stelios Heracles was merely exchanging one prisoner for another, the close proximity of dark, watchful eyes forced her to limit her response to a reproachful shake and an artificially bright suggestion.

'I've so many things to ask you. Let's go up to my room where we can talk in private.'

'I'm sorry, *elika*,' her future husband strolled forward to make his dreaded presence felt, 'much as I regret the intrusion, I feel bound to remind you of the many arrangements waiting to be finalised before tomorrow's wedding.' Displaying a mockery that only she could see glinting beneath a screen of thick, dark lashes, Stelios slid an arm around her waist and drew her close against his side as if determined to demonstrate complete possession. When his head bent towards her she was not prepared for his swift kiss, a swooping assault upon her startled mouth that began as a stamp of ownership, then lingered, curiously and gently exploring until he had located the one quivering nerve that refused to be stilled. It was a ruthless attack, found bearable only because she was becoming accustomed to his cruelty, but its effect upon Gavin was obvious when he rounded upon Stelios to snarl:

'When you have had time to get to know my sister as well as a man should know his prospective bride, you will learn how strongly she detests being *mauled*!'

Petra went very still within the circle of Stelios's arm, feeling the angry jump of a muscle as he tightened his hold upon her waist. She wanted to plead with Gavin not to be difficult, to attempt some pretence of harmony with the man who possessed the power to make them dance, jump or bend a knee simply by pulling the appropriate strings, but when she felt herself caught in a crossfire of looks exchanging mutual dislike she knew that the warning, if spoken, would have come much too late.

She tensed, waiting for Stelios's axe of displeasure to fall upon her brother's head, but instead was forced to watch him squirm, made to feel gauche and ill-mannered by a politely drawled pleasantry.

'Thank you, I shall not forget that remark.' The evenness of Stelios's tone contrasted menacingly with the piercing look he directed towards Gavin. 'You and I must also become better acquainted. Perhaps I could introduce you to the art of fencing, my favourite hobby? Nothing gives me more pleasure than trying out a newly-tempered blade, testing its steel to breaking point until I am convinced that the metal has been sufficiently heated to render it flexible; sufficiently cooled to ensure that it will not snap under pressure.'

Petra's heart sank as she recognised what was almost a declaration of war between the two men—one an untempered youth whose blade of emotions lacked the hone of experience on its blunt edges, the other a well tried lance of steel with pointed sting and barbs which she knew from personal experience could be penetrating, painful, and often deadly.

All her protective instincts reared against the threat cloaked in civility Stelios had directed towards her brother who was still suffering the effects of rough Greek justice. Tomorrow, once marriage vows had been exchanged, she would be honour bound to side with her husband. Today, however, her first duty was towards her weary, despondent-looking brother who felt his freedom had been gained at the cost of an unfailingly supportive sister.

'I'm sorry, Stelios, but Gavin's needs must come first.' Her rebellious decision seemed to take him completely off guard. Taking full advantage of her surprise initiative, she twisted out of his grasp and ran to fling a protective arm around her brother. 'After all,' she dared to mock sweetly across a dividing yard of no-man's-land, 'a bride is entitled to expect the support of a happy, well rested relative at her wedding. I know, Stelios darling, that while I'm seeing to my brother's comfort you can be relied upon to resolve any last-minute problems with your usual flair and efficiency!'

She tugged at Gavin's arm. 'Come with me, dear,' she urged, panicked into retreat by dark eyes smouldering a warning of angry retribution. 'First, you must have a warm, relaxing bath, then, if you feel up to it, we'll have a quiet lunch together in my room.'

'That sounds marvellous, Sis!' Gavin's downcast mouth widened into a grin, but instead of responding to the pressure of hands urging him to flee he stood his ground just long enough to cast a glint of triumph towards the gaoler whose custody he so obviously resented. 'It will be like old times,' he tilted defiantly, 'with just the two of us together. As Father often used to say, the company of a dumb animal is preferable to that of a man whose outlook one finds completely alien!'

Expecting a furious outburst from the volatile Greek, Petra hurried Gavin up the steps of the castle, pausing on the threshold just long enough to cast a furtive glance across her shoulder towards the man standing rigid as a Colossus— and projecting the same presence of petrified power.

She was shaking with reaction when they reached her room, so fraught with nervous tension that Gavin's loud chortle of satisfaction set her teeth on edge.

'That brief contretemps should serve to set the record straight,' he crowed, collapsing into the nearest comfortable chair. 'Who does the guy think he is—some resurrected Olympian god possessing the divine right to boss mere mortals around and to subject *you* to the sort of discipline imposed upon Vestal Virgins! You may have decided to knuckle under, meek sister, to have agreed for some unaccountable reason to allow him to become your keeper, but I have not and most certainly never will! At the first opportune moment I mean to escape from this medieval fortress, and if you have any sense at all you'll come with me.'

Suddenly Petra's sorely tried patience snapped. As much to her own surprise as to his, she rounded upon his lounging figure with eyes sparkling ice-blue fury.

'When are you going to grow up?' she demanded furiously. 'Have you learnt nothing at all from your spell in goal? Stelios has gone to a great deal of trouble to arrange your release, yet instead of showing gratitude for his kindness you've adopted an attitude of truculence, demonstrated contempt of his authority in the most stupid and ill-mannered way! Surely you realise the importance of impressing him with your willingness to co-operate? You *must* obey his orders, or else run the risk of being returned to goal!' She stamped her foot in an orgy of frustration. 'Without your passport you can't leave the island, so there's no place to run where Stelios won't find you.'

'There's Grandfather's house,' he reminded her sulkily, looking very much like a spoilt child whose most ardent admirer has suddenly deserted him.

'Yes, there is,' she nodded agreement, exerting great control upon her peculiarly threshing emotions, 'and you would be safe there, because Stelios is completely unaware of Grandfather's existence.'

'You mean you haven't invited him to your wedding?' For the first time ever she suspected the presence of a speculative gleam in eyes she had always considered candid.

She nodded. 'I've kept our visit to the island a secret from him,' she admitted sadly. 'Patera Romios is too old and frail to have to cope with the shame of knowing that his grandson has fallen foul of the police. Have you no compunction about disturbing an old man's peace of mind?' she challenged gently.

Angrily, Gavin jumped to his feet to bluster a response to her dare.

'As I've already explained, I've done nothing to be ashamed of! But I'm beginning to wonder, Petra, if you're as honest as you pretend. It strikes me as very peculiar that my level-headed, super-intelligent sister should suddenly have decided to throw her bonnet over the windmill by agreeing to marry an arrogant Greek who can hardly be other than a virtual stranger! What beats me,' he frowned, then decimated her pride with brutal candour, 'is why the beast of Buffavento should want an inconspicuous mouse as his bride!' Blind to her humiliated wince, he continued pondering: 'Impoverished Greeks are as noted for their tendency to marry a dowry as are rich Greek tycoons for their penchant towards youthful wives of outstanding beauty. As you fall into neither category, I ask myself what is it Heracles wants that only you can supply. And more important still, what power is he wielding to make you anxious to marry *him*?'

In spite of having been force-fed with indigestible facts pertaining to her lack of sex appeal, Petra managed to choke back angry truths that would have goaded his tempestuous temper into an even worse display of rebellion.

'Thank you for the vote of confidence,' she husked ironically. 'Obviously, you have a very low opinion of my ability to attract any man's interest. Fortunately,' she cleared her tight throat to make room for the lie, 'there is such a thing as the attraction of opposites. As I once read somewhere, people who resemble each other are quick to make friends, but mostly it's complete opposites who fall in love.'

'*Love!*' he hooted with disbelief. 'If it's love that's prompted tomorrow's debacle then you really do deserve sympathy, Petra, because I'm quite convinced that to Stelios Heracles marriage represents no more than intercourse between tyrant and slave!'

'Then I must be the sort of slave who clings to her chains,' she rebuked with dignity, 'for I find little to choose between pandering to the whims of a demanding husband and being constantly at the beck and call of a selfish, spoilt younger brother. It's becoming clear to me that when I tried to fill the gap in your life left by the death of our mother I did you a great disservice, Gavin.' She sighed, forced to acknowledge the logic of Stelios's argument. 'A child that's never allowed to risk a fall or a bumped head developes a false sense of security, an ignorance of life's dangers that breeds a bravado lacking in those who've suffered knocks and bruises, who've fallen flat on their faces and found no one rushing to pick them up, set them back on their feet, and kiss better all their sore places.'

Her newly discovered guilt was almost expiated by the shamefaced look that clouded her brother's features, and by the mumbled statement that gave her grounds to hope that her reprimand, though too long delayed, might not be altogether too late.

'I say, Sis, you're coming on a bit strong, aren't you? I admit to being thoughtless and irresponsible at times, but no more than others of my generation!' Awkwardly, he shuffled his feet. 'In my own defence, I must plead to being an average, normal guy when measured by a conventional yardstick.'

His pained objection brought a flash of insight that made Petra quick to apologise to the boy whose immaturity seemed more pronounced only because she had begun comparing him with the powerful, overbearing strength of one particular man.

A rush of remorse sent her rushing to envelop his boyish shoulders in a reassuring hug. 'Forgive me for the harsh things I said—I don't know what came over me,' she pleaded tremulously. 'I think ... I think perhaps I'm suffering pre-wedding nerves.'

For a brief second Gavin's mouth held on to its sulky pout, then as if stung by the reminder of her earlier accusations, it widened into a forgiving grin.

'I'm not surprised,' he teased with a return of his usual good humour. 'Any girl brave enough to take on Stelios Heracles is entitled to indulge in hysterics!'

A reminder of Stelios as she had last seen him jabbed her conscience. Suddenly she found herself pleading:

'Gavin, would you mind very much if I left you to lunch alone? Greek marriage customs are complicated and prolonged, preparations began immediately the date of our wedding was announced and each day since there has been some different ceremony enacted. Yesterday, for instance, Stelios and I called at every house in the village carrying a gourd filled with wine that had a ring of pastry decorated with tiny pigeons slung around the neck. As each individual was invited to the wedding, he signified acceptance by drinking a little of the wine and eating a small piece of the pastry ring. People living in neighbouring villages have been sent handkerchiefs, silk ones for the numerous *koumeres*—the bridesmaids—and simple cotton ones for ordinary guests. I've no idea what's been arranged for today,' she frowned uncertainly, 'but as Stelios was so insistent that I should join him, I think I'd better do so.'

Feeling an urgent need to make up to Stelios for her slight, she took a step backward and turned to run towards the door.

'Good lord, Petra!' Gavin's mocking laughter followed her. 'I can't imagine you participating in peasants' folk practices. Have you forgotten that you're still a member of the restrained, dignified, and very proper Diplomatic Corps?'

'I'm not—not any longer!' Lightly, she tossed the bombshell over her shoulder as she reached the door. 'So please don't ever refer to it again. Oh, and by the way,' she confounded him with the afterthought, 'don't be surprised if you should hear me referred to as the schoolteacher. That's what everyone thinks I am, so stay on your guard, don't give the game away—and especially not to Stelios!'

Her feet seemed barely to make contact with the ground as, lifted on a wave of totally illogical high spirits, she sped out of the castle into gardens ablaze with bougainvillea, roses, and geraniums daubing blood red splashes against a backcloth of dark green cypress trees, towards the distant sound of violins, mandolins and the soul-stirring rhythm of the bouzouki. For days past, preparations for the wedding had been carried out to the accompaniment of music and song. Every villager, man, woman and child, had been carting trestles and chairs; table linen, crockery, glasses, wine and food to be cooked in huge iron cauldrons set around the perimeter of a circle formed around a marble fountain which centuries previously had been erected near enough to allow its cool water music to penetrate the peaceful interior of a small family church.

A puzzling far-off thudding sound caused her footsteps to falter. Slowly she advanced towards a belt of trees and as she gradually drew nearer she began identifying many deep-throated masculine voices counting in unison with the methodically thudding beat of sound.

'Fifty-seven ... fifty-eight ... fifty-nine ... *sixty*!' As, curiously, she ventured near enough to distinguish each urgently stressed number, the ground seemed to reverberate beneath her feet, a sensation that might have accounted for the sudden buckling of her knees which forced her to clutch for support a tree trunk fringing the edge of a natural arena.

It was filled with an intent, admiring audience, yet was not too crowded to deny her the sight of Stelios stripped to the waist, wielding an axe with a precision and vigour that was causing globules of sweat to trickle down his glistening torso. A breath of wonder caught in her throat as she marvelled at the stamina and strength of his athletic body, at the sight of muscles rippling smoothly beneath dark satin skin as he tackled the test of chopping a

sodden tree trunk into planks under the heat of a
Greek high summer.

As he aimed rhythmic blows in pace with
chanting voices his features were set grimly, as if
he were concentrating body and mind upon
expunging an inner tempest of fury. Petra clung to
her support, feeling weak and apprehensive,
suspecting that she might be the cause of his anger,
yet thrilling to the spectacle afforded by a perfect
physique in the peak of athletic condition
providing proof of strength and determination to
meet all the conditions laid down before a man
could claim his bride.

She realised that he had managed to achieve his
aim when, after one last mighty blow, he threw
down the axe and straightened to cheers of *'Yia
asa!'* yelled from the lips of his admiring audience.

She quivered, feeling threatened by blatant male
virility when he shouted in reply:

'Sto thiavolo ola! Fere krassi! To hell with
everything! Bring on the wine!'

Startled half out of her wits, Petra turned on her
heel to run, not realising that she had already been
spotted until a flagon of wine was pressed into her
grasp and playful hands began pushing her
forward until she was directly in front of Stelios—
a cringing mortal at the feet of an Olympian god.

The silence of expectancy fell all around them as
Stelios stared hard into her eyes before reaching
for the flagon. Supporting its weight upon the
crook of his elbow, he lifted the spout to his lips,
then leant back his head to drink deeply. For long,
thirsty seconds the strong column of his throat
rippled and pulsated in time with her nerves that

had been aroused to a state of panic by a glint of devilment in his vengeful eyes. She stood petrified while he drained the flagon dry, then realised the form her punishment was to take when he tossed it aside and with a lusty whoop of triumph stooped to pluck her into his arms and carry off his prize.

Shocked by the suddenness of his move and almost deafened by roars of masculine approbation, she clung limp as a silken sash across the width of his bared chest as she was borne swiftly out of sight and hearing of their highly entertained, wildly applauding audience.

Breathtaking, turbulent minutes passed before fear began transcending the shock of being kidnapped, carried off in triumph by a silently padding prowler whose sinuous movements, smouldering eyes, and warm heated breath seemed typical of a bloodthirsty animal intent upon appeasing a lusty appetite.

'Put me down!' Desperately she began struggling. 'Where are you taking me . . .?' She pounded his chest with clenched fists, but his only reaction was a growl of laughter, complacent as a purr.

'Are you beginning to regret your dangerous move to undermine my authority?' he menaced softly. Slackening his stride to a standstill, he loosened his grip to lower her feet to the ground.

'You have courage, I'll grant you that!' He smouldered a look that was almost admiring across her pale, apprehensive features. Keeping her shoulders pinned between his palms, he simmered: 'Why do you allow your brother to use you as a cripple uses a crutch? He is a spineless coward who stood nervously by while you jumped into water far out of your depth, allowing you to swim against the stream though fully aware of its punishing current.'

Petra quivered as if physically struck by the threat contained in the indictment that seemed to rise to the height of surrounding trees, shivering still leaves into a fretful rustle, whispering through tall grasses and clumps of wild flowers with heads drooping on slender stems as if oppressed by the surrounding weight of antagonism.

Feeling torn in two by loyalty to her brother and by an illogical sense of duty towards the man who—after hours of agonised thought—had forced her into accepting his proposal of marriage, she choked bitterly:

'Aren't you equally guilty of showing a coward's propensity towards gratifying a base desire to oppress? You accuse Gavin of preying upon my emotions, yet haven't you been just as careful to choose a victim whom duty and compassion has rendered defenceless?' Prodded by despair, she stamped her foot in a burst of condemning anger. 'It's so unfair that qualities of physical strength and aggressiveness should be the prerogative of men who are mostly lacking in sensitivity, who are overburdened with a conceit that leads them to believe that their sex is born into the world wielding a whip designed to thrash tigerish females into submission, make them sheath their claws and, they hope, fawn over and lick the boots of their brutal tamers!'

Fierce Greek sunshine struck sparks of silver from hair dampened by sweat into a tightly curled fleece when he threw back his head and laughed.

'Forgive me, *elika*,' he mocked without compunction, 'but it is hard to picture you prowling tigerishly around any man's bedroom!'

He jerked her forward, taking her so much by surprise she stumbled into arms that hooked her close enough to feel sunwarmed pelt beneath her cheek, close enough to hear and feel threatened by his whispered, deep-throated purr.

'Timid kittens should be confined to nurseries, Perdita—little lost one. Just this once, I am willing to overlook your attempt to scratch my pride by allowing a brother to usurp the position of privilege that ought to be the exclusive preserve of your future husband. But I warn you that tomorrow, my bride, I shall be claiming all a bridegroom's privileges. Basically, my race is not sentimental about weddings—indeed, originally the word wed meant "a pledge", the bride's price which was handed over to the bridegroom by her father.'

'Like a seller in some market place . . .!' Petra managed to gasp, even though her senses were reeling from the effects of his earthy, magnetic proximity.

'Not in our case.' He tilted her chin until she could see the glint of steel in his eyes. 'Marketplace merchants begin with an impossibly high price, working on the premise that the buyer will settle for less. A wife who has promised to provide me with children is what I've bargained for, *elika*! We wed tomorrow on the understanding that that promise will be kept—that you will be neither hoping nor expecting that I might be persuaded to settle for less!'

CHAPTER EIGHT

THE clearing in front of the church was a hive of activity. Stunned by the weight of intent she had recognised in Stelios's softly breathed words, Petra could muster no resistance against the hand manacling her wrist, pulling her towards the crowd of revellers who were laughing, chatting, teasing, sipping ouzo and brandy as they carried out the final preparation of food for the wedding feast. Excited children were running wild, weaving in and out of a circle formed by simmering cauldrons, keeping a safe distance away from naked flames yet now and then pausing to hover hungrily, sniffing the tantalising aroma of pork and chickens stewing in savoury gravy.

Musicians rendering an idle accompaniment to the hum of many voices broke into a wildly strumming warning of their appearance, then waited until the shouts of welcome had died down and the bride and groom-to-be had been seated before leading the villagers into a traditional pre-nuptial song.

In a bemused daze, Petra suffered the possessive grip of Stelios's arm around her waist as they sat side by side on a wooden bench watching village youths performing yet another of their traditional marriage rites, another link being forged in the weighty, unbreakable fetter that was to chain her to an uncaring husband for the rest of her life.

Young girls and boys kneeling on rugs spread upon the ground were turning small stone mills, laboriously grinding grain into a fine powder. Violins began to play, and as the muted melody drifted over their heads the youngsters started singing softly:

> 'Good hour, kind hour
> and blessed hour,
> May the work we have begun
> be a secure one.
> The mountains grew dark
> and they could not finish their feat,
> come along, my girls,
> and let us grind the wheat.'

Intensely moved by the sweet melody accompanying the labour of love, Petra blinked back an onrush of shamed tears, wishing she had sufficient courage to jump to her feet and explain that the elaborate preparations were a waste of time, a mockery, that no amount of ceremonial rites could change the forthcoming marriage into anything other than a sham.

'When a full sackful of the *resi*—wheat for the wedding—has been ground, it will be put into wooden troughs to be carried by the young men of the village to the fountain,' Stelios murmured, playing the loving bridegroom to perfection by placing his lips close against a flaming velvet earlobe. 'A procession of villagers will follow to form a singing circle around the fountain. Then the girls will take over, washing the *resi* seven times before it is added to the meat inside the cauldrons and left to cook all night over a very low fire until required for tomorrow's wedding feast, when the meat will have melted completely, resulting in a tasty savoury dish with the consistency of porridge.'

All the pent-up emotions that had been festering inside of her during the past traumatic days— resentment of the manner in which he had accepted her heartbroken surrender to marital blackmail without so much as blinking an eyelid; bewilderment at having been put at the mercy of physical impulses she could neither control nor understand, quivering nerves; waves of trembling, the reaction of a heart that pounded with the frenzied beat of a tribal war chant whenever she dared to contemplate her initiation into the sexual rites of marriage by a husband who was determined that no rein would be imposed upon his fiery Greek passion and who looked upon their union in the cold light of duty—was contained in her low, bitter reply.

'Doesn't your conscience ever rebel against the deceit of allowing simple peasants to believe that they're preparing to celebrate a loving union, instead of merely the revived ritual of sacrificing a virgin in order to appease the wrath of an omnipotent god?'

For the benefit of onlookers he smiled, but in the deep, dark well of his eyes she glimpsed a flicker, a spark almost, flashing a signal to beware.

'My conscience has many tongues,' his thickly lashed eyelids flickered, 'but the loudest one of all tells me that it cannot be wrong to provide hardworking villagers with an excuse to celebrate. However unimportant our wedding may appear to

you, to them it is an event, a rare social activity
that provides a release for their emotions, a break
in the monotony of working for a living that is all
too short for the amount of feasting, dancing, and
social visiting that has to be crowded into the
meagre time allotted. So please try to smile, *elika*.
Then everyone will be convinced that the
celebrations are not to be wasted upon an
unhappy bride—and I mean *everyone*,' he stressed,
'including your brother! There is a belief held by
the occupants of mountain villages that has
probably been inherited from ancient tribes of
ancestors who made a practice of carrying off
wives from neighbouring villages: *'Marriage is
often followed by many funerals'*.

'Even today, though secretly, and kept hidden
from officialdom, it is not unknown for vendettas
to erupt between villages—to the detriment of
both communities. Though your hot-headed
brother constitutes no threat to my peace of mind,
it would be to his advantage,' he drawled the
warning, 'if you were to attempt to convince him,
both by word and deed, that there is no reason
why our marriage should initiate a blood feud!'

Petra's heart sank. Unknowingly, he had just
given her one more reason why her grandfather
should be kept in ignorance of her marriage. If
Patera Romios were ever to discover that a
member of his family had been threatened or
coerced, neither poverty nor age would prevent
him from exorcising fierce family pride by
unleashing his contempt upon the powerful owner
of a castle with turrets rearing high into the
rarefied region of legendary Olympian gods!

Suddenly, as if supplying a signal to the expectant crowd, Stelios rose to his feet with a shout of, *'Fere krassi!* Bring on the wine!'

With an enthusiastic roar the revellers responded to his cue and seconds later it appeared to Petra as if the boisterous, fun-loving Greeks had gone wild. As the foot-tapping rhythm of bouzouki music filled the air, every man present rushed into the centre of the clearing, stomping and bellowing, leaping, slapping and clicking his fingers in time to the music, hastily refuelling with quick swills from bottles and glasses being tendered by an audience of admiring wives.

'Yia sas, kyrie!' The grinning village butcher approached carrying a bottle and three glasses which he filled to their brims.

'Eiva proti! Cheers to the first drink!'

Stelios lifted his glass and to Petra's shocked dismay downed its contents in a couple of convulsive swallows.

Not to be outdone, the butcher followed suit. Then with smacking lips and madly twinkling eyes he refilled the glasses and responded.

'Eiva thefteri! Cheers to the second drink!'

Aghast at what was apparently the beginning of a contest to prove which of the two men possessed the greatest resistance to alcohol, Petra sat rooted as the process was repeated.

'Eiva triti! Cheers to the third drink!' Stelios challenged, downing his drink without a pause.

'Eiva sto boukalli! Cheers to the *bottle*!!!'

Obviously determined to keep pace, the butcher, whose cheeks had become tinged with an unbecoming flush, filled the glasses once more, then with a flourish of bravado hurled the empty bottle into a nearby clump of bushes.

When a flood of enthusiastic men began hurrying to join them carrying bottles and chairs, Petra began inching timidly away from Stelios, who seemed to have become so vitally involved in the contest that he had completely forgotten her existence.

By the time she had edged far enough away to feel the rough edge of the bench beneath her fingers she was on the perimeter of a vociferous crowd of men apparently dedicated to toasting everyone's antecedants and descendants.

'Here's to your mother ... father ... brother ... sister ... aunt ...!' Then as she was sidling out of sight, a loud and glorious, 'Sti yia yia su ke sta kokkala tis'—here's to your grandmother, and long may her bones rattle!'

She fled as if chased by a crowd of devils towards Sophia, whom she could see in the distance, supervising the positioning of troughs similar to the one she used to burn charcoal, eager to leave behind an atmosphere she found strangely frightening, a build-up of masculine aggression by men eager for mirth, laughter, wine and eventually—the thought caused a panicky breath to flutter in her throat—for equally fruity female companionship!

The youngsters of the village were still absorbed in the important task of cleansing the wheat at the fountain, surrounded by singing children and their mothers. Musicians were playing madly, trying their utmost to outdo the lusty cries of men who had gravitated from the dancing arena to join in the drinking contest. A group of seven kneeling girls crouched low over some secret object on the ground collapsed into a paroxysm of giggles as she sped past. But Sophia, when she reached her, was scowling, her features shaded darkly as shadows being cast by the sun dipping slowly behind the mountains. The object of her displeasure was a young manservant who was paying only minor attention to her scolding.

'No, you may not leave what jobs remain until the morning, I shall not sleep tonight unless I'm certain that everything is ready! In any case, you are far too young to help the *kyrios* celebrate his last night as a bachelor. Before you become eligible to join in such a spree you must have time to gather knowledge or wit—for wine bestows neither!'

'Sophia . . .' Petra began tentatively.

'Oh, *thespinis*!' Impatiently, Sophia shooed away the crestfallen youngster. 'I was wondering what had become of you! At such times as these,' she tossed a scornful glance in the direction of the noisily chortling men whose toasts were becoming more slurred and incoherent by the minute, 'women cannot be blamed for wondering whether it is better to live with men or without them. A jewel of gold in a swine's snout is the role Greek wives are forced to play,' she snorted. 'There's nothing so stubborn as a man who is determined to make a fool of himself!'

The slight criticism of her employer contained within the generalisation struck Petra as so unusual she wondered aloud.

'You must be tired, Sophia, after working hard

all day. Please rest for a while. Sit with me and take time to enjoy a glass of cordial.'

For a moment Sophia appeared tempted to protest, then with a sigh she gave in to weariness.

'Very well, *thespinis*.' She glanced towards a row of covered trestles. 'The macaroni is ready to be popped into the oven; the vine leaves have been stuffed and the meatballs prepared. Only the *bonbonnières* need finishing off, but that is a task that can be completed while we are enjoying our drinks.'

Petra almost achieved a state of contentment as she sat with Sophia sipping rose cordial, watching the creep of evening shadows into the clearing while lazily she placed a selection of sugared almonds into twists of cellophane and tied them securely with gold thread. But the escalating sounds of revelry, the clinking of bottles and the occasional splintering of glass began jarring upon the peace of early evening, causing her nerves to tense, her toes to curl, and her cheeks to flame with embarrassment when increasingly ribald snatches of conversation became audible during intervals when musicians rested, leaving short, silent pauses.

'Don't allow such ignorant remarks to alarm you, *thespinis*,' Sophia consoled dryly. 'Greek-Cypriot males are notorious for fighting fiercely in defence of family honour, nevertheless, in spite of their handsome appearance, in spite of having been reared on the island of love—the birthplace of Aphrodite—most of our mountain men are extremely shy, dependent upon wine to loosen their tongues and to rid them of inhibitions. Even the *kyrios*, who is said to be capable of seducing a woman in seven different languages, has shown uncharacteristic signs of strain today—snapping at the servants, refusing to eat . . .'

Her shoulders lifted in a giant shrug. 'Perhaps in common with the average young Cypriot male, he uses his macho image to hide a nervousness of deep commitment. However,' she nodded sagely, 'I'm certain that tomorrow, during the ceremony, when he knows that all eyes will be upon him, he will demonstrate his willingness to shoulder marital responsibilities.'

'He will?' Petra questioned faintly. 'How . . .?'

'You must listen carefully,' Sophia explained, 'for a moment of great importance that occurs somewhere in the middle of the service. The priest will say '. . . and woman shall fear man.' Those words act as a signal to the bridegroom to step on to the bride's foot in a display of power—not painfully, you understand,' she hastened to assure her, 'just firmly enough to demonstrate dominance, to stress his intention to master.'

Despondency settled upon Petra like a cloud. She had no wish to talk about tomorrow, nor did she even want to think about the sacrificial ceremony that was drawing so terrifyingly near.

'I'm going home,' she told Sophia, too weary to realise that already she had subconsciously accepted Buffavento Castle as her permanent abode. 'I'm feeling tired, I think I'd better go to bed early, otherwise tomorrow's celebrations will be wasted upon a hollow-eyed bride.'

'No, *thespinis*, you cannot!' Sophia surprised her by rearing to her feet, looking agitated. 'Both you and the *kyrios* must be present when the final pre-nuptial ceremony is performed.'

'Not another one!'

Sophia stepped backward, obviously upset by the exasperated edge to her tone, but Petra was beyond caring. Much as she hated the thought of snubbing the kindly villagers, she knew that just one more rite added to the load that had been carried upon her shoulders all day would strain her endurance to the limit. 'I'm sorry, Sophia, but I must go. I . . .' she spun aside, gulping back a heartbroken sob, '. . . I just can't take any more!'

Before Sophia could be given cause to wonder why tears should be pouring down the cheeks of the girl fortunate enough to have been chosen by the *kyrios* as his bride, Petra almost ran in her haste to gain the cover afforded by a dark belt of trees dividing the clearing from the solitary stretch of moonlit garden surrounding the castle.

A shaft of light beaming from one isolated ground-floor window seemed to follow her movements like a baleful eye as she mounted the castle steps. The massive main door was unlocked. Nervously, she began hurrying across the silently brooding hall—then almost screamed with fright when a door was flung open, spilling a beam of light across her path.

'Where the devil has everyone disappeared to?'

She relaxed with relief at the sight of Gavin glowering from the doorway.

'I've been mooching around the castle for hours—left without company, without servants, and consequently without dinner!'

Hurriedly she attempted to placate his foul

temper. 'I'm sorry, Gavin, it's my fault, I completely forgot to warn you that food was being served out of doors this evening! The servants have been busy all day preparing dishes for tomorrow's wedding feast. If you'd care to make your way down to the clearing——'

'No, thanks,' he interrupted as rudely as a petulant child. 'The local peasants may have been easily hoodwinked, but I'm still not convinced that your marriage to Heracles gives cause for celebration.'

Avoiding his narrow-eyed stare, Petra stepped past him into the room, reminded of the imperative need to act upon Stelios's warning. Praying that her voice would remain steady, that hot, aching tears would remain at bay, she forced herself to exercise a growing skill in the art of deception.

'Why must you persist in voicing suspicions of the motive behind my marriage?' she tilted bravely. 'I know you consider me lacking in sex appeal, that you doubt my ability to hold the interest of any man as attractive to women as Stelios undoubtedly is. But it was *he* who chose *me*,' she reminded him raggedly. 'If Stelios is happy with his choice why can't you be?'

'Happy . . .?' Gavin echoed incredulously. 'How can I be happy at the thought of seeing you married to a man who affects you in the same way that a stoat affects a rabbit every time he walks into your presence! Are you asking me to believe that it's natural for a woman to appear terrified by the sight of the man she's supposed to love—and conversely, for the object of her affections to give an impression that most of the time he's unaware of her existence? I've seen the two of you together for just a few short hours,' he raced on, 'but——'

'Just long enough to jump to a series of wrong conclusions!' she flashed triumphantly, knowing that she dared not allow him to carry on, that somehow his thought process had to be diverted from the line of logical reasoning that was leading him towards the truth. 'I don't *care* what you think!' she stressed, fiercely determined to prevent him from becoming a victim of his own curiosity. 'Whatever you may say, however hard you may plead with me to change my mind, I shall still willingly, gratefully, eagerly look forward to tomorrow's ceremony, which will demand of me a promise to stay bound to Stelios for the rest of my life as his loving wife, and, I hope, if God should prove willing, as the mother of his children!'

Even to her own ears her protestations sounded weakly unconvincing. She swept her lashes down to avoid her brother's incredulous stare, hoping to hide the glint of tears, trying to still the working of a traitorously trembling mouth. She had done her best to carry out Stelios's order to rid Gavin of a suspicion that she had somehow been coerced into what he obviously regarded as a potentially disastrous marriage, but as she sensed his angry stare playing around her bowed head she felt certain she had failed. But then, just as her nerve was on the verge of snapping, just as she was drawing breath to start on a guilty confession, he surprised her by responding in a dejected monotone:

'Heaven help you, Petra, I believe you really do love the guy!'

For seconds she was too stunned to register any reaction, but then a wave of relief washed the troubled cloud from her eyes, leaving them brilliant. Forcing her drooping mouth into a wavering smile, she scolded:

'You couldn't sound more depressed if you'd just heard me condemned to life imprisonment! Hunger can often impair a man's judgment—I'll slip down to the kitchen and find out what food is available. After you've eaten, you might find it possible to view the situation in its true perspective.' Quickly, while the tide was still running in her favour, she retreated from an atmosphere seething with the threat of many unspoken questions which she had no desire to be called upon to answer.

The peaceful solitude of the kitchen acted like a balm upon her troubled mind. She searched through the shelves of a cool pantry and found eggs, butter, ham and sufficient left-over vegetables to make a tasty omelette. She was deep in thought, mechanically breaking eggs into a bowl, when the door crashed open and Stelios strode inside the kitchen.

She froze to immobility, directed a startled stare across the width of space dividing her from the tall, slightly swaying figure that had pounced into her hideout, filling it with the coldly glittering menace of a hungry night-time prowler. The sensuous stealth of his advance left her in no doubt that the mood he was in was dangerous. A catch of fear caught in her throat. She began backing away, keeping wary eyes fixed upon lips widening slowly into a smile of savage anger.

'Why did you leave without a word, making me look a fool in the eyes of my companions?'

She felt the solidity of a wall blocking her retreat and pressed her shoulderblades hard against its surface, willing the cold stone to provide some avenue of escape.

'I'm certain that no action of mine has had any direct bearing upon the opinions formed by your friends,' she husked, daring to bait his uncertain temper.

She flinched from hands reaching out as if to paw, then suffered the humiliation of hearing him growl with laughter when he leant his palms against the wall behind her, rendering her captive to tormenting eyes and a heady wine-flamed breath.

'Why are you trembling, Miss Grundy?' he murmured, feathering his lips across a crescent of downcast lashes. 'You make me wonder whether I may have been wrong to resign myself to the prospect of wedding and bedding a straightlaced spinster—a flame without heat—of attempting to slake my thirst with a spirit that appears appealing until one becomes aware of a bitter taste similar to that left by the saccharine you English are fond of adding to sour drinks to lend an illusion of sweetness. I feel an urge to discover whether my judgment was wrong, *elika*,' he confided throatily, dropping his hands on to her shoulders to draw her boneless body close, close enough to make her arch away in panic from the pressure of sheer animal virility.

'Don't be shy,' he coaxed with a fine trace of asperity, 'It is only the first step that is troublesome. Just a few hours from now we will be man and wife—in such circumstances, who could condemn us for anticipating the pleasures we are due to start sharing for the rest of our lives?'

His deep, forceful kiss had a scorching effect upon a body seduced by his persuasive lips into straw-doll flaccidity. Flame flickered, crackled, then razed, blazing an unrestricted trail towards unplumbed depths, burning down barricades guarding secret, hidden places, showering intensely sparking passion along its devouring path.

Enjoy the day; seize the present opportunity, improve the time! Temptation to surrender completely to his wine-inflamed passion was running molten through Petra's veins. She strained nearer, revelling in the crush of his embrace, resting the palms of her hands against his powerful chest as she returned kiss for hungry kiss.

'Hey, Sis, where's that meal you promised me?'

The voice of sanity intruded as if from a long way away. She jerked rigid, but when she attempted to break free Stelios used his body as a shield to press her back against the wall of the alcove that was screening them from Gavin's sight.

'Stay silent and he'll go away,' Stelios mouthed against her ear.

But Gavin's shout had acted like water upon fire, dousing its flaming heart to charred embers, leaving just the slightly smouldering remains of a passionate holocaust.

'Give me a few more minutes, Gavin!' she trembled, surprising Stelios into slackening his hold upon her trembling frame. Smartly, she ducked out of his arms, but was not more than a few hurried steps away when his hand descended upon her shoulder, jerking her to a standstill. Then she was scooped off her feet by arms that tightened with frustrated anger as Stelios carried her towards the door leading from the kitchen into the grounds.

'Make yourself a meal if you want to eat,' he snarled across his shoulder towards her bewildered-looking brother. 'Given luck, you might choke on it!'

Moonlight as bright as day allowed her to glimpse a muscle twitching angrily in his cheek as he strode with her into the courtyard. Desperately she wriggled, trying to fight her way out of arms determined to inflict punishment, then just as she was about to yell a protest the sound of voices drew her attention towards a crowd of amused spectators gathered around the seven giggling young girls she had passed earlier that evening. They appeared to be inserting the last stitches into red ribbons sewn crosswise on to the corners of a newly made mattress, singing words that brought a stinging blush to Petra's already burning cheeks.

Place the four crosses
on to the four corners,
To make the bride and her bridegroom
lie in bed like lovebirds.'

Viced between Stelios's arms and his rock-hard chest, she was forced to watch until the girls had finished dancing seven times around the nuptial mattress. They concluded the ceremony by crossing snow-white sheets over the mattress and spreading them flat before retreating to mingle with the crowd whose chatter had died into an expectant hush.

Grim-faced and unsmiling, Stelios strode forward, then suddenly released his grasp so that she rolled down on to the mattress, turning over several times before coming to rest in a shocked, confused heap.

'Bravo, *thespinis*!' The villagers applauded her dexterous execution of the fertility rite. 'Such a fine first roll across the bridal mattress indicates that the firstborn child of your marriage is almost bound to be a son!'

Vexed and humiliated to the verge of tears, she sat with head bowed until the laughing crowd had dispersed, very conscious of Stelios's shadow looming large as a Colossus as he stood with legs astride, arms folded across his chest, savouring the vengeful satisfaction of knowing that she was feeling cheapened, as deprived of modesty as the notorious females who had walked the streets of ancient Greece wearing sandals that had left imprinted in the dust the shameless invitation: *'Follow me!'*

CHAPTER NINE

Proof that her wedding was to be a gay, noisy, far-from-solemn affair was provided as soon as Petra awoke the following morning. Male voices spilling through a nearby window were singing improvised verses in honour of the bride and groom, some amusing, others raunchy, but all rendered with the same lusty vigour as they had been the night before. Drowsily, she struggled upright, confused by the din made even noisier by Pini's determination to participate, showing his ability to judge when something unusual was afoot by trilling an enthusiastic welcome to early morning sunshine glistening across the wires of his golden cage.

Realisation that the day of her wedding had actually dawned was responsible for the wide-eyed, fearful look Sophia noticed immediately she entered the bedroom carrying a breakfast tray laden with a coffee pot, fruit, sesame buns, and a jar of rich golden honey.

'At last the day has arrived for everyone to respond to the invitation, "*Kopiaste ston gammo tis koris mas*"—come to the wedding of our daughter!' She bustled towards the bed wearing a beaming smile. 'The mothers and daughters of the village have begun stirring and beating the *resi*. Your *koumeres* are all assembled downstairs giggling nervously as they wait to be called upon to carry out their duties of combing and dressing the bride. And as you have no doubt heard,' she concluded dryly, 'the *koumbari* are noisily engaged in their task of shaving and valeting the bridegroom.'

'How many valets does a bridegroom need?' Petra attempted to scoff but somehow managed to sound timidly plaintive. 'Judging from the noise issuing from the *kyrios*'s room there must be a dozen or so men inside.'

Nodding agreement, Sophia set the tray down upon a bedside table. 'It is customary for the groom to have a retinue of male companions—a throwback from the days when a bridegroom "won" his bride by carrying her off against her family's will, having wasted no time in wooing either her love or confidence. Abduction died out, and as times grew more civilised the groom's raiding companions became known instead as *koumbari,* bachelor friends who groom and attend the bridegroom at his wedding. Which is probably just as well,' she scoffed, bending to plump up Petra's pillows, 'for after the amount of wine that was drunk last night I doubt whether any one of them is capable of defending the groom against angry male relatives descending in a body to snatch back the unwilling bride!'

Petra collapsed against her pillows, knowing exactly how earlier brides must have felt, feeling that centuries had rolled back to the days when wedding had meant abduction and man's choice of bride had been governed by revenge, material gain, duty to procure an heir to his family fortune— anything other than to be united in love, to

become part of the fusion of two separate entities
into one devoted couple, two hearts beating as
one.

'Make haste, *thespinis*!' Sophia's plea penetrated
her misery. 'Finish your breakfast while I run your
bath. Greek bridegrooms frown easily if their
brides keep them waiting at the altar!'

But a few sips of coffee were all Petra was able
to force down a throat made increasingly
constricted by the blast of masculine voices
escalating to the heights of ribaldry. Abandoning
all attempts to eat, she threw back the bedclothes
and ran to close the windows, trying to shut out
the sound of Stelios's laughter as he responded to
his companions' jokes in the manner expected of
the leader of a pack of virile stags.

'Don't listen to them, Pini,' she murmured
sadly, feeding crumbs of sesame bun to the pet
who demonstrated his affection by pecking her
finger. 'Sons of Adam are formed from dust,
which could explain their earthy eagerness to crack
a chaste sheet of ice beneath their heels; to stamp
clumsy footprints upon a blanket of pure white
snow.'

'Your bath is ready, *thespinis*.' Sophia bustled
out of the bathroom and cast a disapproving
glance over the untouched breakfast tray. 'In ten
minutes' time I shall return to see if you are ready
for the *koumeres*, who are waiting to help you to
dress.'

The prospect of having her privacy invaded by a
horde of giggling bridesmaids was sufficient to
impel Petra towards the bathroom, determined to
bath, shampoo her hair, and to slip into at least

her underwear unaided. She accomplished her tasks so swiftly and with such a lack of bridal concern that when Sophia returned as promised she found Petra seated in her petticoat in front of a dressing-table, smoothing a hairbrush across a flow of shoulder-length hair toned down by dampness to the sheen of dark Greek honey.

Startled into swifter action by Sophia's reappearance, Petra abandoned the hairbrush, drew two fistsful of hair towards the nape of her neck, then began twisting it tightly back from her forehead into its customary coil, leaving her head seal-sleek, lending a cool marble purity to her cameo profile.

'No! No! Sophia clasped her hands together to add urgency to her appeal. 'Please don't do your hair that way—not today!'

'Why ever not?'

When Petra swung round to direct a look of astonishment the old servant's cheeks flushed, but bravely she stood her ground.

'I intend no disrespect,' she mumbled. 'It's just that, today of all days, your bridegroom should be allowed the pleasure of seeing you as I do each morning, with your beautiful hair tumbling past your shoulders, forming a soft golden frame around features tender as a child's, lacking all trace of the severity you employ as an oyster employs a shell to secrete a pearl. Man is a conquering beast,' she confided wisely, 'a male whose pride is at its most rampant on his wedding day. Always, he expects a bride to delight the eyes and excite the envy of his friends—and it is to a woman's advantage that this should be so,' she coaxed slyly. 'As well as being proud, the male sex is by far the more sentimental. In spite of his notorious reluctance to make such an admission, it is a well known fact that a man's first glimpse of his bride on their wedding day becomes a memory that remains with him for ever—acting as a spur upon his conscience whenever he feels tempted to stray; blunting the edge of his temper on trying days; reminding him of the need for tenderness and patience when hot blood is urging him to have his way!'

Petra blushed crimson. Since the day Stelios had won the contest of wills by forcing from her a promise to marry him, she had deliberately avoided dwelling upon the physical aspect of their union. But Sophia, in a way that was typical of a race that idolised physical perfection, whose mythological characters included Circe, the sorceress, and Apollo whom they worshipped as the personification of youthful manhood, had brought home to her in full force the ordeal of sex without love which very shortly she would be called upon to face. In the circumstances, Sophia's advice appeared sound. Stelios's coldly calculating attitude towards their marriage might soften if the colourless nonentity he had chosen as a wife simply because of her ability to fade into the background of his life should turn out to be pretty and appealing . . .

'Very well, Sophia,' she sighed, 'I'll leave myself entirely in your hands. You may tell the *koumeres* that the bride is ready for their attentions.'

Five minutes later her bedroom was filled with chattering, excited bridesmaids jostling for the honour of dressing and grooming the bride. Her dress, that had been offered as payment in kind by the village dressmaker whose daughter had been enrolled as a prospective pupil, had been designed along traditional lines of peasant simplicity, swirling, roughly textured cotton that was sufficiently diaphanous to demand the modesty of a fine silk beneath its gathered folds.

As it was drawn over her head to settle with a rough sigh over curvaceous breasts and slender, tapering thighs, a collar of delicate Lefkara lace lifted in the draught, then settled into a circle of overlapping petals around her pale, slender stemmed neck. She submitted patiently while two of the bridesmaids brushed and combed her hair until a stream of honey gold was flowing on to her shoulders and tumbling in fine swirls round her forehead and against cheeks glowing pink with excitement.

The girls sang softly as they executed tasks elevated to artistry by frequent repetition.

> 'Do adorn her well, the pearly one
> to whom her mother hath given every
> eight days a bath,
> and whom her father
> hath bedecked in gold.'

'The bride is now ready for the sash, Sophia!' Laying down the brush and comb, the girls urged Petra to her feet as they continued singing.

> 'Call her mother too
> to come and tie her sash
> and bless her
> and then give her away.'

Tears were streaming down Sophia's cheeks as

she advanced towards Petra carrying a bright red ribbon. The sight of her sadness caught Petra emotionally off guard. She swallowed hard, bracing herself to withstand that part of the ritual usually undertaken by the bride's mother, who was expected to shed tears for the daughter about to leave her sheltered home to meet the strenuous demands of a husband who was almost a stranger. She stood motionless while Sophia fumbled blindly with the sash, then when she eventually managed to tie it around her waist she smiled at the tearful old servant and bent to place the symbolic goodbye kiss upon her cheek.

'*Na zisete, thespinis,*' Sophia whispered shakily. 'Long life and much, much happiness!' She stepped back to allow the bridesmaids to position a white lace headkerchief on Petra's head, then with her hands clasped together she nodded to the smiling bridesmaids and breathed ecstatic approval.

'*Kalliste*—the most beautiful! The bride is now ready to meet her bridegroom.'

But immediately Petra joined Gavin who was waiting at the foot of the castle steps to escort her to the church all her cool courage deserted her. Not even Gavin's incredulous stare, the jerked exclamation that was a compliment in itself, managed to bolster the weakness of her trembling limbs.

'Good lord, Sis, I never once suspected that your prim disguise was hiding such a reserve of beauty!'

Two children, each carrying a huge white candle, fell into step beside them as they proceeded towards the church. Directly behind them was a small girl carefully carrying a tray holding wedding wreaths and two golden rings tied with ribbon the colour of the bride's sash—red, the colour of joy. Behind her came the chief bridesmaid, who was also carrying a tray containing a glass of red wine, a glass of oil, and saucers filled with bread and cotton seeds. The retinue of bridesmaids formed up behind, completing a colourful procession that wended slowly behind Petra until she entered the clearing in front of the church, when they dispersed to mingle with a crescent of wedding guests curving towards Stelios and his *koumbari* who were lined up on each tip of the half-moon to form a complete circle.

The air was filled with the delicious smell of spitted lamb and poultry; savoury, slowly simmering *resi;* and small, nutty, oval-shaped wedding cakes that had been individually baptised in rose blossom water, rolled in icing sugar, then left to waft their scent in the air while they dried. But as Petra stepped into the circle of wedding guests she was conscious only of the overpowering perfume of sweet basil, and the equally potent impact of a bridegroom exuding the virility and strength of Heracles himself, dressed in the traditional wedding garb of black breeches, embroidered shirt, and with a gleaming dagger thrust into the red silk sash circling his waist.

Stelios started forward at the sight of his bride, then stopped suddenly in his tracks. As Petra lifted her eyes to meet his she felt a small thrill of triumph, the pleasure known only to one who had seen an enemy completely disconcerted. Yet predictably, in spite of dark eyes questioning her ability to emerge like a butterfly from a chrysalis, he was quick to recover his composure.

He held out his hand, silently commanding her to cast off the chains binding sister to brother, then when nervously she obeyed by sliding her small, cold hand into his, he began escorting her towards the church, drawing her close to his side so that only she could hear his whimsical murmur.

'Change of name, change of identity? Is that the sort of reasoning that has led to your amazing transformation? Your Miss Grundy title may weigh heavy, but by discarding its protection I fear you may have left yourself as vulnerable to danger as a hedgehog stripped of its needles!'

Little of the tiny weatherbeaten church with its slanting roof of dark brown tiles, that had been built solely for the use of the Heracles family and the villagers of their feudal estate, registered upon Petra's mind. Even the interior left her with no more than a blurred impression of painted walls, one depicting a particularly apt tableau of Doubting Thomas with a couple that could have been a bride and bridegroom kneeling at his feet. As she was being led down the aisle towards an altar she glimpsed a carved, gilded *iconostasis* incorporating a bird nibbling grapes, and behind that a selection of old religious relics; processional crosses, and an icon painted upon a crescent-shaped canvas. The air smelled sweet with a mixture of perfume from banked-up flowers; smoke rising from wicks fitted into bowls filled with oil, and from candles composed of multi-

coloured pieces of wax glowing in flickering
flamelight like miniature stained glass windows.

She waited calmly by Stelios's side until the
shuffling feet of villagers piling into pews behind
them were stilled, but when a priest approached,
signalling them to kneel to receive his blessing, the
realisation that she was committed to sinning in
church, to exchanging deceitful vows and promises,
set her trembling violently.

She endured the service as she would have
endured a nightmare, consoling her troubled
conscience with the assurance that very shortly
she would waken, that the children proffering
beribboned rings; the partaking of bread and wine
during Holy Communion; the cottonseed confetti
that was thrown during the service while, hand in
hand, she and Stelios were led by the priest three
times around the altar followed by *koumeres* and
koumbari holding on to long white ribbons
attached to the wedding wreaths, were all part of a
fantasy, a wildly imaginative dream.

She chanced a glance towards Stelios when the
priest began reading a passage, and felt a rise of
anger at the sight of his mildly amused composure.
'. . . *and woman shall fear man . . .*'

She heard the priest intoning the words Sophia
had quoted, the signal used by the bridegroom to
demonstrate power over his bride. She saw
Stelios's foot rising, then without stopping to think,
without daring to consider the consequences, she
swiftly lifted her satin-slippered foot to stamp a
pointed heel down hard upon his instep.

An audible ripple of amusement from the
congregation brought her to her senses. With

cheeks flaming, she lifted fan-spread lashes to allow fearful blue eyes to seek his reaction, then looked quickly away from the sight of a mouth registering tight-lipped disapproval, from lean cheeks turning a pale shade of pain beneath dark tan, from eyebrows beetling over eyes sparking a threat of early retribution.

Outside the church liquid gold sunshine simmered as fiercely as Stelios's tightly controlled anger, a cauldron of resentment and injured pride that was stoked up to boiling point by jesting, unrepentant *koumbari.*

'Stelios, poor Stelios! Your reign of authority is over!' shouted one of the most audacious, casting a challenging look towards companions who were doubled up with laughter.

Stelios's grip tightened around her arm, delivering bruising insight into the true state of his temper as he forced himself to respond in a jocular vein to teasing comments that were thrown thick and fast as confetti as they walked towards decorated tables set around the clearing.

'If your heart was quite set upon a crown of thorns, you did well to choose one made of roses, Stelios, for at least its pretty appearance should help to make its prickles more bearable!'

'Never mind, *kyrie,* at least you were given time to learn how to command before being forced to obey!'

'It makes a change to see a mare throw a saddle over a rider!'

'Drink a farewell toast to freedom, Stelios. From today onwards your life threatens to become a little garden with a straight and narrow path!'

Stelios's smile had been reduced to the tight baring of lips over clenched teeth by the time they reached the 'first table' which they were intended to share with the priests, the village elders, and their retinue of *koumeres* and *koumbari*. Much to the lessening of Petra's inner agitation, jesting gave way to sincere expressions of, *'Na zisete*—Long life to the happy pair!' as guests lined up to shake the hand of the bridegroom and to accept their commemorative *bonbonnières* of sugared almonds from the pale but surprisingly beautiful bride.

By the time everyone was seated, numerous toasts had been drunk, and feasting was about to begin, Stelios managed to address her in a tone that sounded almost affable. Guests displaying hearty appetites were tucking into a selection of grilled meats and savoury dishes, but to Petra's dismay she and Stelios were served a dish reserved especially for the bridal couple. Tensely she stared down at the offering on her plate, feeling heartbroken affinity with the tender young bird that had been plucked, trussed and slowly roasted in order to tempt the approval of a jaded appetite.

'You must eat a little of your pigeon—our guests must not be offended by the sight of a bride rejecting a dish that is considered a symbol of a life of love,' her bridegroom drawled unkindly. 'Consider yourself fortunate that tradition has been relaxed far enough to allow the dish to be included in the wedding feast. As a rule, it is served for breakfast on the morning after the wedding night, once the bridal chamber has been inspected by the bridegroom's parents, who expect to be provided with proof that the marriage has been properly consummated.'

Petra shrank from his first barbed counter-attack, from the hostility she had aroused the moment she had squashed his pride beneath the heel of her silken slipper, and felt a rush of gratitude towards Sophia for insisting that her hair should be left loose, providing a silken screen for cheeks blazing red, the colour of joy—and of humiliation.

She sat without stirring, feeling his dark eyes penetrating her flimsy defences, then received further indication of his unforgiving mood when, with an unkind hand, he brushed aside her flimsy screen, baring her blushing discomfort.

'Eat, Petra,' he menaced, pitching his tone low enough to be drowned by the swell of conversation and by the drift of sweet, romantic music being coaxed from violins, '. . . or chance providing me with a fortuitous excuse to demonstrate publicly that my status of authority remains unaltered, that my bride, in spite of her attempt to prove otherwise, still occupies a position of subordination!'

His words sounded like a threat to force-feed her, mouthful by mouthful, with the flesh of the tortured bird!

Her stomach retched, but she picked up her fork with trembling fingers, then, hiding distress behind a crescent of lowered lashes, she lifted a tiny morsel of meat to her lips. She gulped, and managed to swallow it whole before the taste had time to taint her tongue, nevertheless her feeling of revulsion was so strong she felt compelled to lift her head and direct a dumb appeal for pity from eyes darkened into deep blue pools of torment.

She felt she had never hated him more than when he laughed aloud, flexing muscles of superiority. Then she experienced a savagely alien urge to strike him when, judging victory to a nicety, he withdrew from further conflict by engaging a guest in conversation, content to leave his sickened adversary choking on the taste of defeat.

The celebration continued all day and right throughout the evening, hours upon hours of eating and drinking, with everyone dancing off their excesses and renewing their appetites, with the exception of the bride and bridegroom. Petra felt chained to Stelios's side, her every move to escape frustrated by his grasp upon her shoulder, by clinching fingers around her wrist, by arms stamping a brand of possession around her slender, red-sashed waist.

But when the celebrations had reached a late-evening peak of merriment, and Stelios was finally persuaded to join his *koumbari* in a male exhibitionists' dance of strength and virility, Petra seized the opportunity to go in search of Gavin and found him sitting alone, brooding into a glass containing the last remaining drops from an empty wine bottle propped drunkenly against the leg of his chair.

'So the bride has at last been reminded of old family ties!' he greeted her sourly. 'No doubt you're feeling in need of sensible companionship, for the only act missing from this performing circus is the ritual of guests pinning paper money on to the dress of the bridal puppet! But then,' he sneered, 'gifts of money to the wealthy Stelios Heracles and his bride would hardly be appropriate. How pleased I am that Grandfather has been spared the agony of watching his adored granddaughter decked out like a *houri* eager to become part of a sultan's harem! Can't you just picture him now,' he challenged, tipping back his chair until his weight was uneasily balanced upon its two hind legs, 'sitting on the well-worn straw seat of one of the "village chairs" spilling out on to the pavement in front of the coffee shop, blatantly interrupting his cronies' intense political discussions, ignoring their gestures of resignation, in order to boast once again about his incredibly superior granddaughter whose intelligence has gained her access into a world previously confined to the authoritative male—the granddaughter whose outspoken opinions about female emancipation never failed to leave him gasping. Tell me, Petra,' he righted his chair with a savage thump, 'how can you relate your present situation with the release of women from bondage, oppression, and legal, social, and moral restraint? How can any person who used to be so strong an advocate of the emancipation of slaves bring herself to participate in a marriage that offers to the bride no more freedom than is offered to a convict who has to serve his term?'

She flinched from his acid condemnation, from his cruel reminder of the grandfather she adored, the elderly patriarch whose fierce expression and inflammable temper hid a heart of pure silver, as soft and abundant as his crop of tightly curled hair. Inevitably, her decision not to tell him, much less invite him to her wedding, would inflict hurt upon the proud old man whose response to every enquiry about his health and wellbeing was a philosophical shrug, followed by the dry assurance: '*Eh, pernoune zoune*—I get by. I survive.'

The thought of his hurt was so unbearable that Petra stammered an assurance designed more to reassure herself than Gavin.

'He'll understand. Once I've explained the situation, he's sure to understand . . .'

Gavin leapt to his feet to hiss with a venom that only a man possessing a strain of Greek blood can instil into his language:

'*Sto thiapolo,* Petra!'

'Do take his excellent and opportune advice, *elika.*' The sound of Stelios's voice ringing sharply as steel sent her spinning in search of his threatening presence. 'Your brother has just advised you to go to the devil.' He executed a mocking bow, then straightened to fling his arms out wide. 'Come, *kalliste*, it is not wise to keep the devil waiting!'

The ebullient, fun-loving *koumbari* were engaged in the old Greek custom of relieving high spirits by smashing piles of plates to smithereens as Stelios guided her, unnoticed, away from the clearing and towards the looming, deserted loneliness of the castle.

She strove to project an outward semblance of calm, to allow her cold, captured hand to remain as still as the frightened little bird he had cupped in his palm, but beneath her unruffled mien she was feeling as heart-thumpingly terrified as Pini must have felt, as trapped, as helpless, as completely dependent upon her gaoler's mercy.

Stelios made no effort to speak as he led her across a hall whose dimly lit interior seemed laden with oppression, then up a marble staircase with steps so cold they appeared to freeze to the thin soles of her slippers, causing her feet to drag, her knees to buckle beneath the strain of approaching a summit offering no protection from complete exposure. When they reached the top she faltered, raising anxious eyes over his implacable features for some sign of warmth, some hint of softening.

But the look he returned was pure Greek in its gambler's determination to collect everything that was due, in its passionate, deeply implanted desire to mount the winner's rostrum and collect the golden accolade awarded to a winning competitor.

'You *have* to take a prize, haven't you, Stelios?' she condemned huskily. 'Your entire existence is directed towards winning, whether it be a wager, a war, or merely a game.'

A lantern swaying gently in a draught cast a sliver of light across shadowed features, igniting in the depths of his brooding eyes a flame that seared her very soul. Petra shrivelled, feeling sacrificial flame licking around her feet, sensing that she was about to be engulfed by the passion of a man who regarded her not so much as a wife as a stand-in for Gaea—the deep-breasted goddess who had been worshipped as the universal mother, who had been said to have created the universe and to have borne the first race of gods and the first humans, the supreme goddess by whose benevolence men had been blessed with fair children and all the pleasant fruits of earth . . .

'Until this moment, it had not occurred to me to

liken our marriage to a game, *elika*,' he murmured throatily, stooping to lift her from her feet to carry her, limp as a golden-haired doll, in his arms. 'But I am not averse to viewing life as a playground— so long as there are toys provided for all ages!'

CHAPTER TEN

ALL the sights and sounds of the village passed
Petra by as she wandered with her head downbent
along the main street towards the classroom which
every morning for the past three weeks had been
filled with eager children dressed in uniforms of
Greek-flag blue, long-sleeved 'aprons' belted over
their regular clothing to form bulky outfits that
they were required to wear throughout their years
of schooling.

Deep in thought, she passed beneath vine-
covered balconies overhanging the street full of
houses outside which villagers were going about
their daily tasks—a black-robed grandmother
using a hand-mill to grind wheat used for making
soup; a grizzly-haired grandfather re-stringing a
mandolin; a farmworker riding a donkey through
narrow alleyways leading towards fields spread
over the slopes of the mountains; a silkmaker
winding thread into hanks; women weaving cloth
on ancient looms; tending batches of bread baking
in communal ovens; enjoying a gossip while they
waited their turn to fill water jars from a leisurely
trickling spring.

'Kalimera, kyria!'

Petra's head jerked upward as she was startled
back to earth by the friendly greeting. Then
immediately she blushed, embarrassed by the
kindly yet speculative appraisal of women too

astute not to have guessed the reason why the *kyrios* had married her rather than one of the parade of beautiful girls they had become accustomed to seeing being ferried towards the castle in the passenger seat of his car—fragile, flirtatious, glamorous girls whose vain, pampered existences had rendered them unfavourable candidates for motherhood.

'*Kalimera,*' she husked, trying hard not to mind the blatant curiosity of villagers whose lack of modern conveniences had resulted in the development of a closed community where privacy was unheard-of and where everyone's affairs—like communal ovens—were regarded as property to be publicly shared.

Confirmation of the direction in which the women's thoughts were drifting was supplied by the wife of the village grocer whose attempt to sound offhand caused Petra's mouth to curl upwards for the first time in days.

'How is your little *kanapini*?—the puff of yellow feathers whose trilling is loud enough to keep even an infant awake, as no doubt you will shortly discover for yourself, *kyria,*' she concluded with a heavy, meaningful stress of humour.

'Pini has completely recovered from his ordeal. His singing is constant and rather loud,' Petra admitted ruefully, 'but so far no one has complained of having had their rest disturbed.'

'Then make the most of this tranquil period,' another woman broke in, grinning widely, 'for once your first child arrives there will be no such peaceful existence. Each day, the women of the village are taking turns to light tapers from the candle that is always kept burning in the church, and offering up a prayer that the *kyrios's* wish for a son will soon be granted. As each taper burns low another is lit, so that in the silent dimness there remains a tiny, flickering symbol of hope—a constant reminder to worshippers to include yourself and the *kyrios* in their prayers.'

Petra swayed, rocked by an unbelievable wave of pain that had swept through her sensitive body, the pain of hearing put into words the basic reason for her presence in Stelios's mountain retreat, the *only* reason why she had been allowed to share his bed, to creep into his arms, to pretend that he was as much in love with her as she was with him.

Somehow, she managed to take her leave of the keen-eyed women without appearing too shaken, without betraying the heartache that had been her constant companion for more than a long, lonely, deserted week. She hurried on her way, anxious to find some haven of solitude in which she might compose her thoughts, control her trembling limbs, before facing a classful of demanding pupils. Blinded by tears, she turned off the main road and stumbled down a steep path leading towards the river and the ruins of an ancient mill almost smothered by encroaching greenery—tall trees towering above the roof of its ramshackle structure and down towards a picturesque stone bridge so rarely used it had become covered in grass and a profusion of delicate lilac-coloured flowers.

'A long time ago,' the children had confided, 'the beautiful sound of bells used to ring a musical accompaniment while the mill did its work.'

As she slid down on to a grassy bank to rest her aching head against cold grey stone forming an archway over tumbling water, she imagined she could hear once again distant pealing, sweet and joyful as the response made by her heartbeats whenever Stelios entered their bedroom. With a moan of deep unhappiness she leant against the screening stonework and gave in to the relief of tears, trying not to dwell upon the cause of her misery, yet unable to prevent her thoughts from reliving yet again the wondrous, breathtaking happiness she had discovered during the first two weeks of her marriage.

With tear-blurred eyes fixed upon the river she stared sightlessly, picturing in her mind's eyes an image of herself on her wedding night, nervously awaiting the arrival of her bridegroom. She had been standing shivering by the side of a huge, unfamiliar fourposter bed, divided between the prospect of creeping between its covers, thereby running the risk of appearing too eager, or of allowing Stelios the first sight of his bride wearing a wedding gift that had been woven by the skilful fingers of an old silk-maker before being passed over for cutting and stitching into the delicate hands of his equally skilful wife. But before her frantically confused mind had had time to form a decision Stelios had marched out of an adjoining dressing-room wearing a silk robe glowing rich and red as passion. Abruptly he had checked his approach, his air of unconcern betrayed by an audible gasp of appreciation when he had glimpsed her near-nudity, an outline curving smooth and pale as wax beneath a shimmering, diaphanous cloud of silk.

'Kyrie eleison!' he had blasphemed in a whisper. 'How do you manage such an aura of untouched purity? You are much cleverer than I had imagined, little lost one,' he had drawled, quickly recovering his composure, 'but your attempt to make me feel as if I am about to commit an act of desecration must not be allowed to succeed!' In a couple of strides he had moved close enough to arouse a panic-stricken pulse in her throat. 'A wife has no right to impose upon her husband the guilt of a thief prepared to steal a blessed candle from a place of worship!'

Yet if she had been a candle, Petra mused painfully, an object made entirely of wax, she could not have melted more readily beneath his touch, could not have been so swiftly set alight by the flame of passion that had caused glowing heat to penetrate deep inside her, melting all resistance, leaving her soft, warm, pliant, eager to be moulded into whichever shape or pattern he found most pleasing.

For two idyllic weeks Stelios had continued teaching her the art of loving, appearing regularly each night to share her bed, to kiss, to caress, to murmur, to tease—but never to stay.

Until their last night together, when he had appeared unable to tear himself away.

Petra had awakened the following morning to discover him still sleeping beside her with a protective arm cradling her to his chest. She had had confidence enough then to tease him awake by dropping featherlight kisses upon a chin made to look dark and piratical by overnight shadow, then had squealed a protest and tried to evade a retaliatory lunge that had brought rasping bristles in contact with her tender skin.

She stirred uneasily, tears of humiliation welling into her eyes as she relived the thrill of his softly-growled laughter, the wicked threat he had whispered roughly against her ear.

'Very well, *yinéka mou*, if you insist, I will wait until night time for the blanket of darkness all shy young kittens seek before lapsing into savagery!'

Yet after that period of contentment and surpreme happiness he had shunned her completely, leaving her to wonder and weep in her lonely bed, finding what little consolation she could from the knowledge that she had never quite managed to nerve herself up to the point of whispering the shy confession that she had fallen deeply in love with her tender, solicitous, passionately possessive husband . . .

Years spent practising self-discipline, together with a strong sense of duty, finally prodded her out of her morass of misery and on to her feet. Her pupils would be waiting—probably fidgeting and fighting to alleviate their tedium—for her to make an appearance. It was not fair to force them to share in her rejection, to make them suffer as she was suffering because the man who had taught her all about loving had grown bored with his pupil.

The first person she saw when she reached the main road was Zeus, the boy with the mischievous eyes whom teasing classmates had christened 'teacher's pet'. He was hurrying in the direction of his home, stuffing a bright blue smock inside his satchel as he went. Immediately he caught sight of her he jerked to a standstill, looking ludicrously dismayed.

'Because you were so late arriving, class has been dismissed, *kyria*,' he almost accused, then bent his head low to continue addressing his shuffling feet. 'My friends and I had planned to go fishing . . .'

'Then don't let me stop you,' Petra encouraged gravely, realising that her pupils were also in need of some fresh distraction. 'On such a day as this the fish will almost certainly be biting!'

The boy's stammered words of gratitude followed behind her as she turned and began walking in the opposite direction to the school-room, feeling a mixture of contradictory emotions—relief at having been spared the effort required to instruct keen, intelligent pupils, and regret that during a period when she needed to be kept busy she had been left with time on her hands.

Aimlessly she wandered along the cobbled streets of the village, finding new surprises around every other turning. Villagers called out greetings as she passed, elderly women pausing in their task of sifting pulses—beans, peas, lentils and *mahos* which were used in place of fresh vegetables during the long winter months—young girls sewing dowry linen allowing her to examine and admire their exquisite embroidery; wives enticing her with the smell of freshly baked bread hanging in large string baskets to cool, tempting her to accept the honey-spread slice that she was offered.

But her greatest surprise of all was the sight of Gavin engrossed in conversation with a saddle-maker who was sitting crosslegged on a rug with the tools of his trade spread around him. She started guiltily, conscious that during the weeks since her wedding she had had little time to spare for her brother. Tentatively, she approached him from behind, nerving herself for a display of resentment or at the very least, sarcastic reproaches.

'Gavin . . .!'

His head spun round, and as he rose to greet her she saw that his features were creased into a harrassed frown.

'Hello, Sis!' Her tension relaxed. He sounded weary, yet reluctant to abandon an absorbing occupation. 'I'm sorry I can't stop to talk at present,' he swiftly confirmed her theory. 'My task for today is to make a detailed study of the method used to make saddles. The saddlemaker intends moving on as soon as his work is finished. He travels all around the island making and mending, staying at each village just long enough to attend to his customers before moving on to the next. I'm finding research into ancient trades and customs very interesting,' he surprised her with the admission. 'If only your husband wasn't such a hard taskmaster I might even find it enjoyable!'

He raked his fingers through his hair, looking highly aggrieved. 'Each morning Stelios hands me a list of subjects he wants me to research, then demands a progress report that has to be ready on his desk before dinner each evening. I wonder if he has any notion how much effort is involved in chasing people up, encouraging them to confide the secrets of their craft, in studying, questioning, and writing up notes! Take today, for example,' he exploded hotly, 'for hours I've sat here watching the saddlemaker at work, taking careful inventory of the tools used—large scissors; a distaff; three different sized needles, a horn stuffed with oil-soaked cotton wool which he employs to force stuffing into the layers of the saddle; asking why it's necessary for the horn to be stuffed with cottonwool and discovering that it's the only material that keeps the oil in the horn without allowing it to dry up! It will be hours yet before he's finished layering the saddle, yet after he's gone I shall have to find time to research the second item on my agenda. There'll be hell to pay,' he assured her in a tone laden with the dread of past experience, 'if the notes on both subjects aren't laid on Stelios's desk, neatly typed, ready for his attention before dinner this evening!'

Petra's heart swelled with indignation as she noted his weary look of frustration; his dust-streaked, sweated brow. A suspicion that Stelios might be punishing Gavin for her own shortcomings prompted an impulsive suggestion.

'Let me help you out. School has closed down for the day, so I've plenty of time to spare. What's the second subject you have to research?'

'*Soujoukos,*' he breathed hopefully, 'some sort of sweet usually made by elderly ladies for their grandchildren.'

'In that case, Sophia is bound to know everything there is to know about it. While you're busy with the saddlemaker I'll go and ask her,' Petra decided. 'Then when I've gathered all the available information I'll type out the notes and leave them in Stelios's study. If we both remember to be careful,' she breathed in deeply, her courage faltering, 'there's no reason why he should learn anything about my involvement.'

She found Sophia busy in the kitchen, weighing and measuring ingredients for yet another of the dishes which she cooked so superbly.

'One *oke* eggplants . . . one *oke* ripe tomatoes . . . half *oke* of mincemeat,' she murmured, double-checking items spread out upon the table as she expertly wielded a chopping knife through a bunch of fresh green parsley.

'Are you too busy to talk, Sophia?' Hopefully, Petra hovered on the threshold, reluctant to interrupt the queen in her kitchen.

'Of course not, *kyria!*' Sophia's smile encouraged Petra to advance a few steps towards a chair placed next to the kitchen table. 'In just a few more minutes I shall have finished preparing lunch. I hope you will enjoy my *papoutsakia ston fourno*—"little shoes in the oven".'

With a gurgle of appreciative laughter Petra assured her: 'I know I shall, Sophia. Both my brother and I look forward to sampling local delicacies made as only you can make them.'

It was a genuine compliment—not extended solely to flatter—yet Sophia's gratified response provided Petra with the opening for which she had been searching.

'Though I do say so myself, there are not many cooks left on this island who are capable of preparing dishes exactly as they were prepared in the old days. I've even heard it said,' she snorted with disgust, 'that some so-called chefs employed in luxury hotels dare to offer visitors dishes prepared with dried herbs sprinkled out of a packet! What on earth must their guests think of such supposedly traditional dishes?'

'Not much, I guess,' Petra nodded agreement. 'Traditional methods are fading fast, and will soon disappear completely. The *kyrios* is so concerned about this that he has asked my brother's help to compile a record of ancient crafts and customs, practices that were once common to the island but which are nowadays confined only to the mountain villages. The making of *soujoukos*, for instance . . .'

'Ah, yes!' Sophia laid down her knife, her interest obviously aroused. 'As a child the *kyrios* so much enjoyed sitting around the fire on winter evenings nibbling the nutty confectionery while I told him tales about the *kalikantzari*, small gnome-like creatures who come down to earth on Christmas Eve and roam around the villages after midnight doing all sorts of mischief—teasing weary home-wenders, frightening the womenfolk, stealing food, and playing all kinds of practical jokes. If ever you should suspect that you might have become a victim of the *kalikantzari, kyria*,' she instructed quite seriously. 'You must scare them away by carrying a black-handled knife, or by twisting a piece of red thread around your finger! On the other hand, if you prefer placating the impish creatures, you must leave a plateful of sweetmeats where they are sure to find them. *Soujoukos* is said to be their favourite.'

Making a mental reservation to leave out a plateful of goodies just in case her present troubles could have some connection with a gnome who had mislaid his calendar, Petra groped inside her handbag for a notebook, then waited with pencil poised to jot down further items of fascinating folklore.

'Shortly,' Sophia did not disappoint her, 'when the vineyards change colour and grapes are waiting blue-black or yellow on the vines, village women will begin cleaning their cauldrons or having them newly lined with zinc. Roofs will be swept clean, and also every patch of sunny courtyard where raisins can be spread out to dry. Children will be given the job of cracking nuts and stringing the kernels into long necklaces which they will tie to forked branches, ready to be dipped into grape jelly in much the same way as they dip their fishing rods into the river. Meanwhile, large cauldrons of grape juice will have been brought to the boil, sweetened with a handful of "white earth", then taken off the fire so that the froth which forms can be skimmed away. After it has cooled, the juice will be strained through a cloth, thickened with flour, then put back on to the fire to boil until it has reached the consistency of jelly into which the eager children will be allowed to dip their strings of nuts several times until they take on the appearance of strings of sausages. These will then be hung up in the sun to dry and some days later the *soujoukos* sausages will be cut into lengths and stored away until winter, when it will be nibbled in the evenings—a sweetener for the mouth that provides pleasure and nourishment for the children.'

'Strange,' Petra mused, too absorbed in her scribbling to realise that she was wandering on to dangerous ground, 'I cannot recall my mother ever mentioning *soujoukos*.'

'How could your mother have had knowledge of

a sweet that is peculiar to the mountain villages of Cyprus?'

When Petra looked up she saw Sophia eyeing her thoughtfully. 'One guest, who was present at your wedding only because she happened to be visiting relatives in the village, seemed convinced that she had seen you and your brother many times before, *kyria*. She even went so far as to suggest that you might have relatives—a grandfather, I think she said—living in her own village which is situated not far from here on the lower mountain slopes. Of course, we assured her that she was mistaken,' Sophia frowned, her lips pursing doubtfully, 'for how could she be speaking the truth, what possible reason could you have for deceiving the *kyrios* who introduced you into his household as a stranger?'

Feeling a childish urge to snatch up a black-handled knife as protection against mischief making *kalikantzari*, Petra jumped to her feet and managed to avoid responding to Sophia's tentative enquiry by stuffing the writing pad back into her handbag and pretending to have suddenly gone deaf.

'Thank you so much for your help, Sophia.' Nervousness caused her to stammer as she began backing out of an atmosphere of hurt disbelief, from a look of rigidity on Sophia's features that seemed indicative of deep shock, and even deeper disapproval. 'I can't wait to tell my brother about the interesting information you've supplied—such a large amount that I shall be forced to spend the entire afternoon transposing barely decipherable scribbling on to neatly typed pages.'

She escaped with relief into the castle gardens, regretting the slip of the tongue that seemed to have opened floodgates of doubt in the mind of the elderly servant whose first loyalty would always be tendered towards her beloved *kyrios*.

She walked for a while between flowered borders, enjoying the warm stroke of sunshine upon hair which Stelios had insisted must be left loose, so that whenever he felt the need he could stroke his hand across a sheen he had likened to the glint of pale sunlight upon a stream of rich Greek honey.

She had also started dressing to please him in gathered skirts and matching tops made of soft striped cotton fashioned by the village dressmaker in a range of jewel-bright colours that had an effect upon her pale cheeks that was positively glowing. Today, she had chosen a dress with a silken amber sheen that had the sort of low, scooped-out neckline so much favoured by precocious young peasant girls who loved to flirt with their eyes across one bared, rounded shoulder, then pretend to be offended by the hot lingering stares of susceptible males.

'But what good is a play without an audience?' Petra murmured to herself as she turned her steps towards the castle and the hours of work that were waiting.

Feeling certain that Stelios would once more have followed his week-long routine of driving away from the castle early in the morning, and remaining absent for the rest of the day, she made straight for his study where she knew she would find a typewriter. But the moment she slipped inside the book-lined room she sensed his presence, felt her eyes drawn as if magnetised towards the outline of his head and shoulders rearing above the padded leather back of an armchair.

She froze, then began silently backing away from his finely drawn profile, his motionless body, and from hands restlessly fingering the traditional male-Greek toy known to some as a prestigious sign of leisure and to others as worry beads.

'Don't go, *elika*!' He startled her by swivelling his chair around to face her. For a couple of stress-filled seconds he studied her fiery-cheeked confusion, then continued in an indolent drawl that somehow managed to sound more disturbing than a threat: 'It is time for us to talk, time to sort out the problems that concern us and which consequently can only be resolved by us.'

CHAPTER ELEVEN

SLOWLY, feeling a need to touch him that was almost compulsive, Petra moved into the centre of the room, then stood nervously clasping and unclasping her hands while Stelios strode around the desk to meet her. She braced, expecting a punishing stab of words from the tongue he used like a double-edged sword that cut both ways, one edge condemning, the other slicing sweetly into her heart, reducing it to a thousand quivering pieces.

Anger aroused during his solitary wrestling with problems she suspected were in some way connected with their marriage seemed slowly to abate as she stood trembling in his shadow, looking pale and drawn but with a new, lovely bloom of maturity softening the planes and hollows of her delicate features.

'Why are sacrificial offerings always so colourless?' he grated the hurtful question. 'Milk-pale calves; snow-white lambs, and pearl-pure virgins.' Suddenly he relented by offering a little less irritably: 'It is customary for a bride to receive a gift of jewellery from her bridegroom, *kallista*— would you prefer pearls, the recognised symbol of purity?'

'And of tears,' she reminded him quietly, then regretted the response that had thrown a cloud over features looking unusually drawn, cast in the grim, weary mould of one who had shared her agony of sleepless nights spent searching for reasons to explain painful solitude.

'I'm sorry if all you have learnt from our marriage is the language of grief,' he apologised grimly. 'You shall have pearls, and when you receive them you must wear them nightly. I shall take care to choose gems that are flawless and white—the holy colour worn by virgins as protection against evil spirits who might attempt to prey upon an unconscious—and therefore vulnerable—sleeper.'

Petra flinched from dark eyes flashing daggers of scorn and felt flattened as the carpet ground beneath his heel when he turned aside, muttering an imprecation so vicious it left her quivering.

'Sto thiavolo ola! To hell with everything!'

As she watched him striding back to his seat an old Greek warning flashed through her mind: 'Poke not a fire with a sword!' Being careful not to irritate him with sharp words that would serve only to increase his rage, she sifted compassion gently as sand on to dangerous flame.

'You're looking tired, Stelios, have you been overworking?'

'Of course I am tired, of course I have been working hard!' Rifling an impatient hand through piled-up papers on his desk, he glared a look of condemnation. 'I retreated from the city to the peace and quiet of the mountains hoping to reduce a backlog of important correspondence, only to find myself becoming more and more encumbered with unforseen distractions.'

Such as an unwanted wife? Petra almost blurted. *One whose too-eager responses have inflicted boredom and embarrassment upon a husband who, by his own admission, considers that catching ends the pleasure of the chase!*

She sighed, dismissing for ever any hope of mating with her husband in thought, purpose, and will, growing with united heatbeats into a single pure and perfect being. Yet even though he seemed determined to reject close communion in favour of a marriage run along the lines of casual recreational sex, she knew she possessed one talent he was bound to find useful.

'Let me help you with your work, Stelios.' She moved towards the desk, viewing its feast of pamphlets, memos, reference books and piled up correspondence with the eyes of a starved child too long deprived of substantial nourishment.

A trace of some undefinable emotion flickered across his features before his eyes narrowed to the watchfulness of a cat standing guard over a dishful of cream.

'Of course you may, if that is what you wish,' he agreed with a smoothness she found faintly disturbing. 'Perhaps you could begin by attempting to interpret the complex terminology employed by the writer of this letter.' He flicked a sheet of foolscap within her reach. 'I am beginning to suspect that our Civil Service has grown into a monument in danger of collapsing beneath a weight of official forms, red tape, and paperclips, and that the officialese used in correspondence is designed not so much to display wisdom as to cover up stupidity!'

Petra almost smiled as she picked up the offending letter thinking, not for the first time, how much he and Sir Joseph had in common, how equally impatient they both were of long-winded officials, pomposity, and all communiqués that were not sent out in as brief and concise form as possible. She scanned the letter, competently unravelling bureaucratic jargon as she went, discovering contents that were blessedly familiar.

In her eagerness to help she did not pause for thought, but embarked upon a verbal de-coding of an obscure point of international law which only a few months previously had overtaxed Sir Joseph's patience. He had passed it into her hands, offering it as a grumpy challenge to her capabilities, a challenge she had found both absorbing and informative.

But immediately she had finished reading, silence fell like a heavy, sinister cloak over the book-lined study. She looked up, half expecting to see admiration written across Stelios' features, perhaps even to hear a grudging expression of gratitude, and instead saw bleak condemning eyes; heard a grated, accusing question.

'Why did you lie to me about your profession, Petra? Why was it so important that I should believe you had trained to become a school-teacher?'

His attack took her completely by surprise. Shocked speechless, she endured his long, deeply penetrating, quite frightening stare with eyes mirroring grave, gentle appeal. But the menace in his movements as he prowled towards her gave clear indication that he was in no mood to consider being merciful—more ready to savage the victim caught in his neatly-set trap.

'You apparently possess a considerable talent for deception, Petra,' he accused coldly. 'Indeed, if acts were angels that walk with us, I suspect that your most frequent companion would be Lucifer!'

His stance was rigid, his expression thunderous, when he directed a challenge across the narrow chasm of space dividing them.

'Earlier today,' he spelled out steadily, 'I received a most informative telephone call from Sir Joseph Holland, a senior British diplomat, who was anxious to know the whereabouts of a girl recently employed by him as his senior secretary, a paragon of intelligence by all accounts, a brilliant scholar, expert linguist, and dedicated career woman who resigned her position in case she should be accused of using her diplomatic status to influence the release of an imprisoned brother.'

Petra's visible flinch at the mention of Sir Joseph's name must have destroyed any lingering doubt he might have been nurturing, even before she quivered a sigh and murmured flatly:

'So you know . . .'

Her damning admission had the effect of a lighted match on a pile of paraffin-soaked charcoal. Slumbrous temper ignited. Sparks of anger seemed to crackle all around her when Stelios' hands clamped down upon her shoulders, jerking her near enough to become aware of his volcanic heartbeat, to feel the scorch of his explosive breath against her cheek.

'All I know for certain is that you have deceived me, Petra! Again and again you have cheated and lied—initially by tricking your way into my office, then afterwards by pretending to be a simple, unpretentious schoolteacher. What a fool you must have thought me! How easily I fell for your line of unsophisticated innocence, the Miss Grundy image you projected with such skilful pathos!'

Savagely he shook her until she felt punished as a puppet in the hands of a crazed master. Yet she felt even physical pain was preferable to the shock of humiliation inflicted by a tongue that lashed.

'I consider the most wicked deception of all to be your act of virginal shyness in the bedroom, your ability to wear the cord and cowl and white silk habit of a saint over the body of a sensuous wanton!'

'*Don't*, Stelios!' she cried out, closing her eyes in an agony of shame. 'You're being unfair!'

'Unfair!' he spat, highly infuriated. 'Have you any notion how debauched you made me feel? How reluctant to become responsible for a virgin's first sexual encounter?' He tossed back his head to direct a bitterly mocking parody. '*Hail, goddess!* Just as legend has foretold, once more the waves have flung forth a shameless Aphrodite!'

When he contemptuously withdrew, leaving her feeling charred to the heart, as, weak and brittle as a wand baptised by flame, she sagged against the desk yearning for the support of Aphrodite's girdle, the mythical *cestus* Greeks believe is worn by all women of irresistible attraction because of its magical power to arouse men's ardent love.

Slowly, painfully, she trembled upright, anxious to escape the heavy silence filling a room that had taken on the ambience of a prowling lion's lair. Step by cautious step she began backing towards the door, keeping her eyes fixed on the back of his black-maned head, willing brooding thoughts to keep his mind occupied until she was out of reach. The sound of her heartbeats was pounding in her ears by the time she had moved to within groping distance of the door. Then just as she began reaching towards the handle, just as she was teetering on her toes preparing to break into a run, the door was flung open by Gavin, who sauntered cheerfully unsuspecting into the lion's den.

'I hoped I might find you in here, Sis!' Momentarily oblivious to Stelios's presence, he handed her a sheaf of loose-leaf pages. 'Here are the notes you offered to type—I'm so grateful to you for undertaking half of my research programme, without your help I wouldn't now be looking forward to a long relaxing soak.'

'Without the help of a nursemaid sister, I doubt whether you would eat, much less wallow in the idle existence you appear to accept as your due!' Stelios almost snarled behind him.

Gavin swung round to face his sharp-toned attacker. Remaining sublimely insensitive to deadly undercurrents, as well as to the lingering pall of animosity left from their recent battle, he made an unfortunate decision to respond in a mocking vein.

'I work hard at being idle,' he flashed an engaging grin. 'In fact, I'd go as far as to say that I'm a dedicated student of an art in which I hope eventually to obtain a degree.'

Sensing smoke signals rising from still-smouldering embers of wrath, Petra tried to prevent Gavin's fingers from being burnt.

'My brother didn't mean that, Stelios,' she

pleaded, her eyes deeply earnest, dark as midnight sky. 'He was merely being . . . flippant.'

'As flippant as a child who has been spoiled by an over-protective nanny,' he agreed with a cold edge of sarcasm. 'It appears to me,' he turned to scowl at Gavin, 'that the art upon which you should be concentrating all your efforts is that of the process of maturing. To become an adult one needs to be left alone to develop the core of inner strength that enables man to survive all setbacks. So, starting from dawn tomorrow, you will continue your studies among the shepherds and goatherds who tend their flocks during summer months on the higher mountain pastures. The length of your stay there,' he pronounced austerely, 'will depend upon the time you take to show convincing evidence that you are ready to carry your own burdens of responsibility, instead of shifting them on to the shoulders of a sister whose obsessive devotion to yourself is beginning to pose a threat to her own identity.'

His shocking verbal douche left Petra gasping, and for a few fraught seconds Gavin too seemed incapable of finding words. He stared at Stelios, his face paling, flushing, then paling again before he managed a defiant refusal.

'If you think you can force me to spend an unspecified period of time among sheep, goats and taciturn shepherds then you can think again!' he challenged rudely. 'Having to live here is bad enough—there's no way you can force me to accept further curtailment of freedom.'

'Oh, but yes, there is,' Stelios insisted with such

a suave intent that Petra was convinced he meant every word. 'I can send you back to goal!'

Every last faint hope of happiness died within her when Gavin stormed out of the room, leaving her at the mercy of a fierce Greek male who, with a few dozen words, could make a friendship—or form an enmity likely to endure for a lifetime.

She had no pleas left in her for Gavin, no excuses or appeals for leniency. All she wanted of her angry flint-eyed husband was an answer to one vitally important question.

'Stelios . . .' she husked, struggling to force painful words past her lips, 'do you really think me capable of simulating shyness? Of . . . of . . .' a blush raced high into her cheeks then sank deep enough to stain her very soul, '. . . being willing to satisfy sexual instinct in the arms of a man for whom I feel no love?'

'I'm not certain what to believe, Petra.' Much to her relief he did not attempt to touch her, but left a yawning gap between them while he forced an admission between tight lips. 'I had begun to think of you as an intensely private person, one excited by small treats, easily moved to tears by distressed birds and animals, dismissive of your natural beauty and of the beguiling charm that made simple villagers take you to their hearts. But a person viewed externally—from outside—often turns out to be completely different from the purely sociable image one has formed. Given time,' he turned aside, looking infinitely weary, 'I may find it possible to resume the duties of a husband. At this moment, however, I feel that the relief I would find most welcome would be news

that procreation has been successfully carried
out—that already you are carrying a child.'

Stabbed numb by his casual treatment of a
subject so sensitive that even gentle discussion
would have left the imprint of a bruise, Petra
slipped quietly out of the study leaving him alone
with his deeply morose thoughts. With the
detachment of an automaton she climbed the
staircase, then walked the length of a passageway
to her bedroom feeling an urgent need to talk to
someone, yet knowing that the only ears she dared
trust belonged to Pini, the little yellow bird who
had been told all her secrets because his tongue
was incapable of betraying a confidence.

She heard his sweet song of welcome immediately she entered a room filled with sunshine—
except for the space occupied by Gavin's hunched
figure. He was standing glowering out of a
window, but turned to face her as if he had been
anticipating her arrival.

'What am I to do, Petra? I must get back to
university for the beginning of term, yet I could
tell from Heracles's expression that he wasn't
bluffing, that he really meant every word he said.
My career's at stake, Sis—with or without your
help I must get home to England!'

'Don't worry, I'll help you to escape.' Petra's
response was automatic, her words echoing in her
ears as if from far away. Even her strange choice
of phrase did not impinge upon her subconscious
as she talked and walked through an intolerable
cloud of pain.

'You will?' Gavin's face cleared. 'I didn't expect
... I hardly dared hope ... I thought that, now

you're Heracles' wife, you would feel it your duty to conform to his wishes.'

Heracles' wife! Feeling a dull ache where her heart should have been, Petra began mentally sorting through a list of wifely designations, seeking a niche that might relate to her own peculiar status. Spouse; partner; consort; soulmate; helpmate; broadwife; housewife—fishwife! No, even that humble term would flatter a wife expected merely to reproduce, to propagate, to be the clinical vessel that nurtured her husband's offspring . . .

'Petra, are you feeling all right?'

Gavin's face loomed through a black mist of misery, looking anxious, as concerned as one who has just become aware that others might have problems even greater than his own.

With an almighty effort Petra dragged her mind back to the present, forcing herself to concentrate upon the task of deciding how to get away from Buffavento Castle, and where to go.

'We must go to Grandfather's,' she decided calmly.

'We?' Gavin's shocked exclamation whistled through his teeth. 'You mean you're coming too?'

She nodded, then without giving him time to spill out questions she could not bear to answer, she began outlining swiftly: 'You'll need your passport, without it you've no hope of leaving the island.'

'It's kept in a drawer of the desk in Stelios's study,' he told her eagerly.

'Good. In that case, we must wait until the coast is clear before attempting to retrieve it. While you're keeping watch, I'll start packing a small suitcase with essential items,' she instructed with the fatalistic calm of a kamikaze pilot, 'it's best to travel light, because I wouldn't be surprised if feet should turn out to be our only means of transport.'

Less than two hours later, after escaping from Buffavento with ludicrous ease, they were trudging the narrow, twisting, pebble-strewn mountain road leading down to the lower slopes where their grandfather's village was situated. Minutes after their plan of action had been formulated, Stelios had unknowingly left their way clear by driving away from the castle in the manner of a man determined to seek an antidote to poisonous thoughts—probably in the company of his many female friends, Petra had decided sadly, whose sweetness might help to counteract the bitter resentment coursing through his veins.

Because they had timed their departure to coincide with the servants' siesta hour there had been no sound of movement, no curious grooms or gardeners to watch or comment upon their hurried exit from the castle grounds.

'This blasted heat!' Gavin grumbled, pausing for the umpteenth time to cock a hopeful ear, willing some sound of approaching transport. But not so much as the clip-clopping of donkey's hooves disturbed the hush of a heat haze pressing like a blanket over a sleeping population. Wearily he set down the suitcase containing their combined possessions to mop a handkerchief over his sweat-beaded brow. 'I know just how a penitent must feel wearing sackcloth and ashes,' he grimaced.

'Ashes to ashes and dust to dust; if God won't have him the devil must!' Then, as if arriving at his subject by the process of word association, he continued without pause:

'Stelios is hardly likely to give up his wife without a fight, devilish pride will send him scouring the island immediately he discovers that you're missing.'

Petra stumbled, then hobbled across the verge to rest on a large boulder, using the need to massage a ricked ankle as an excuse to hide humiliated colour forced into her cheeks by his casual implication that, whatever reason might prompt Stelios to search for his wife, it would not be love.

'I've thought of that,' she murmured painfully. 'Our one chance of remaining undetected is the almost certain possibility that searchers will be told to concentrate all their attention on the airport and seaports. As Stelios is unaware of Grandfather's existence, he's unlikely to suspect us of choosing a hiding-place that's practically on his doorstep.'

'True,' Gavin conceded moodily, dropping down on the verge beside her, 'nevertheless, I'd rate our chances of success a great deal higher if only you hadn't insisted upon bringing that darned bird. The sight of a fair-haired girl carrying a caged canary could be equivalent to leaving a visiting card with every passing villager.'

'I couldn't leave Pini behind,' she choked, her fingers tightening convulsively around the small travelling cage she had previously condemned. 'And please, Gavin, don't go on about stowing him out of sight—he needs plenty of air and the happiness of basking in sunbeams.'

'Hush!' Gavin jerked upright, cocking his head to one side. 'Start saying your prayers, Sis, and hope that the faint rumbling becoming gradually louder is being made by the local bus!'

He had barely finished speaking when an ancient-looking vehicle grunted around a bend, its roof-rack packed with cardboard boxes and baskets piled with produce, its window seats lined with curiously-staring but mercifully unknown faces.

'*Stamáta!*' Gavin leapt into the middle of the road waving his arms and shouting at the top of his voice. '*Stop!*'

Thankfully Petra grabbed Pini's cage and began limping towards the bus that was being wheezed to a standstill by a driver so confident of not being overtaken that he did not bother drawing the bus towards the verge. She stepped aboard, then with as much composure as she could muster began weaving a pathway through sheep, goats, chickens and ear-splitting conversation towards a seat hastily cleared of parcels by accommodating passengers.

'Whatever you do, don't start admiring the livestock,' Gavin muttered in a jocular attempt to coax a smile on to her forlorn mouth, 'otherwise we could leave this bus with the beginnings of a menagerie! Cheer up, Sis,' he urged, settling next to her with a relieved sigh, 'you may have left behind a castle, but shortly you'll be arriving at the next best place to home!'

Yet a stifling hour later, when the bus drew up inside a deserted main square, nothing could have looked less like home or less like the majestic outline of Buffavento Castle than the cluster of grey stone houses with paint-blistered doors set in old-fashioned mouldings; courtyards teeming with browsing chickens; herb-choked windowboxes made out of discarded paraffin tins, and balconies piled with melons left to ripen in the sun.

They waited until the bus set off, returning the waves of friendly passengers until it had disappeared around a bend, then without exchanging a word they began walking through the village until the road turned right, leading them across a strip of olive and carob groves towards a simple house with a ground floor balcony surrounded by a rickety-looking balustrade.

As they crunched along the garden path Petra noticed a stirring of movement on the balcony, heard the creaking of a cane chair, then met a piercing look of enquiry from ancient eyes peering beneath the battered brim of an equally ancient straw hat.

'Patera Romios!' she called out, feeling a sudden aching need of her grandfather's wise counselling and undemanding affection.

'Petra! My little Petra . . .!' He rose to his feet and flung his arms open wide.

Pausing just long enough to thrust Pini's cage into Gavin's hands, she stumbled up the steps and fell, half laughing, half crying, into her grandfather's hugging embrace.

'Oh, Grandfather, I'm so glad to be here with you!' she choked against his broad, comforting shoulder, feeling safe, rescued, as reassured as Pini must have felt when comforted by Greek male strength and tender compassion. 'Why do we have to grow older? Why can't time be made to stand still so that we could always play in the kingdom of childhood where no one is ever deliberately hurt?'

'But would you also wish to forgo an adult's appetite for living, *elika*?' her grandfather murmured, his wise eyes assessing her quivering mouth and eyes that were deep blue wells of unhappiness. 'Achieving maturity can often be painful, but even a bird is forced to peck its way out of a shell before it can ever hope to fly.'

CHAPTER TWELVE

TRUE to the tradition of hospitality practised by open-hearted Cypriots since time immemorial, Patera Romios's neighbours and friends had insisted that the family reunion should be celebrated with a feast. The largest and fattest pig available had been slaughtered, dressed, washed in hot water and rubbed with salt and lemon to whiten the skin, then hauled on to a huge wooden block for the butchering to begin. For days past the women of the village had been working hard preparing choice delicacies, marinading hams in troughs filled with rough red wine, rendering down fat for preserving any left-over pieces of meat, frying strips of skin into crispy crackling, boiling the pig's head and feet for many hours, reducing the meaty liquid so that, when cold, it would set into a tasty savoury jelly.

Yet Petra was finding it difficult to appear cheerful as she sat on the balcony sharing a pot of coffee with her astute, too keenly perceptive grandfather.

'I do wish you could have persuaded your friends not to have gone to so much trouble, Grandfather,' she shifted uneasily. 'After all, the circumstances that gave rise to my unexpected visit call more for regret than rejoicing.'

'So far as my friends are aware, your visit was planned to surprise and delight an elderly grandparent,' he reproved gently. 'I trust they will be given no cause to suspect that I am actually harbouring a couple of fugitives—one from justice, and the other from a newly wedded husband whose displeasure she has somehow managed to arouse!'

Holding the coffee pot poised over his empty cup, Petra paused to direct a stare of suspicion towards the elderly patriarch whose expressionless features and mildness of manner were completely at odds with his excitable Greek temperament. Since early childhood she had grown used to her grandfather's fiery outbursts of temper that was easily provoked, swift to escalate, then just as readily apt to die down. He possessed the volatile nature of a firework, she had often thought, a short-fused thunderflash that soared skyward, ridding itself of explosive sparks before descending safely back to earth. So why had he taken her confession so calmly? Had his explosive core evaporated with age, or was his fuse secretly smouldering, threatening to erupt into a dangerous rocket of resentment?

'I missed you yesterday, Grandfather,' she probed, keeping her tone as casual as she was able. 'It's not like you to absent yourself from the village for an entire day. Where did you go?'

'Er . . . nowhere in particular.' Airily, he waved away the question, then deliberately changed the direction of the conversation by sinking his teeth into a slice of syrupy semolina cake. 'Mm, it's good!' he nodded, twinkling bright-eyed approval from beneath an overhanging thatch of eyebrows. 'You have forgotten none of the lessons taught to you when you were no higher than your grandmother's knee. Do you remember how wise she was, *elika*, how kind, how anxious to preserve the peace? What were the words she used to scold children who quarrelled and refused to make up?'

'Wounds fester and swell in silence,' Petra faltered, slowly setting down the coffee pot. 'It is fatal to be too proud to explain.'

'True. So very true,' he murmured, rising from his chair to wander across to a flower-filled tub spilling blossoms over the rail of the balcony. 'Fable has labelled three paths to hell, jealousy, anger and pride—the latter owing its well trodden surface to the feet of many young lovers.'

Snapping the stem of a poppy between gnarled fingers, he contemplated the drooping head of blossoms cupped within his palm and sadly shook his head. 'It has been said that at one time all flowers grown on this island were colourless. After a misunderstanding with Aphrodite, her lover Adonis went hunting and was gored by the tusks of a wild boar. As Aphrodite ran to help him her feet were scratched by thorns, and drops of her blood stained white roses red. Just as the blood of her expiring lover dyed anemones and poppies the same passion-dark colour. Such a shame,' he sighed heavily, 'when lovers part in anger, blinded by pride, deafened by misunderstandings, often reconciled too late to enjoy the full rich glow of happiness.'

Casting fantasy aside like an unwanted cloak, he suddenly turned on his heel to astound her by declaring: 'You are obviously deeply unhappy, my child. Am I right in suspecting that you are very much in love with the husband you deserted?'

'*Deserted?*' Petra sprang to her feet, distressed to the point of tears by the mere mention of the man whose ghost haunted her thoughts by day and her restless, unhappy dreams by night. 'How like a Greek male to place his loyalties on the side of one of his own sex—however damning the circumstances,' she choked, feeling hurt and betrayed by his seeming shift of allegiance. 'I did not desert my husband. I left him because . . . because I couldn't bear the thought of spending the rest of my life loving a husband who chose his wife as a gardener would choose a propagator in which to sow his seed and nurture a family of seedlings!'

She felt ignored and cruelly let down when, with an inscrutable smile, her grandfather dismissed the argument he had deliberately provoked by observing mildly.

'*Etsi ine i zoi!*—that's life! And now, *elika*, I must ask of you a favour, Patroclos, my oldest and dearest friend, has not been feeling too well lately. I owe him a visit, but because my old bones have been wearied by yesterday's outing, I should be grateful if you would call at his house now—at once—to ask him if he feels able to join in our celebration this evening.'

Five minutes later, having given in to her grandfather's determined persuasion, Petra set off walking along a deserted dust track leading towards a house set a little apart from the rest of the village. A silken breeze rustled through trees falling in graceful swathes from a distant summit crowned by the dazzling pinnacle of an almost hidden monastery housing black-bearded monks whose mystical quality of repose seemed to seep through ancient walls to spread the blessing of peace over the surrounding countryside.

Sunrays played warmly around shoulders left partly bare by the scooped-out neckline of a peasant blouse as she wandered, too painfully numbed for deep thought, through a small orange grove, then up a flight of steps leading to a house with shuttered windows and a door firmly closed, as if its owner was absent or still sleeping.

Three times she knocked, each time a little louder, then when no response seemed forthcoming she frowned, alarmed by the idea of her grandfather's elderly friend being sick and in need of a doctor. Deciding to check the garden and orchards in case he should be working, she walked around to the back and was immediately relieved of anxiety when she spotted a high-backed rocking chair being swayed to and fro by its hidden occupant.

'Kalimera!' she called out, her steps lightening with relief as she advanced to conclude her greeting. 'My grandfather sent me——'

A thunderbolt of shock jolted through her body, rooting her feet to the ground so that she had no option but to remain staring wildly into grave, inscrutable eyes, to rove the planes, hollows and scythe-sharp features of a profile she had thought she would never see again.

'Kalimera, Petra,' Stelios responded softly, easing his lean frame upright. 'Your grandfather is also responsible for directing me to this meeting place.'

'He is?' she responded dazedly, unable to break the link chaining her gaze to his. 'But how? Where? I had no idea that the two of you had even met!'

'Until yesterday,' he simmered, prowling cautiously towards her, 'I was unaware of his existence. Why did you leave so many gaps in your family history, *elika?*' he questioned keenly, halting within reaching distance. 'Why did you leave me so unprepared for the invasion of my home by a fierce old patriarch thirsting to revenge the harm he was convinced I had inflicted upon his granddaughter?'

'Oh, no!' she gasped, backing away from his intimidating nearness.

'But yes,' he nodded, advancing to regain lost ground. 'I quite seriously believe that, had I not managed to convince him that I had been wrongly judged, he would not have hesitated to carry out the duty imposed by the rules of vendetta which state that the nearest kin of an injured victim is entitled to avenge family outrage by drawing blood.'

He seemed content not to touch her, but waited as if ready to spring, watching the progress of horrified emotions chasing across her stricken features, willing her to ask the question that had begun as a faint flicker of query in her troubled eyes before slowly, gradually, developing into the glow of a penitent's candle casting golden shafts of hope into hushed, densely shadowed places.

'Patero Romios is not easily swayed once he has formed an opinion,' she eventually obliged, hardly daring to look higher than the lion's head emblem chained across an expanse of tanned chest left exposed by a partially unbuttoned shirt.

'I have recently been convinced of that fact.' His words stroked soft as silk across her downbent head. 'No convicted criminal could have faced a judge less inclined to be lenient, or have been made to plead his cause more eloquently than I.'

She stiffened to the immobility of a bird unused to gentle handling, unable to believe words breaking quietly into the hot sunny silence.

'It is not an easy task for a man to bare his soul, *kallista,* to confess his mistakes, to admit to fear instilled into a boy who was tragically deprived of both parents, left to grow up lonely and afraid, convinced that close relationships are inseparable from unendurable pain, and consequently deciding to avoid at all cost being manoeuvred into any situation that might leave him vulnerable to yet another emotional trauma.'

He moved, closing the space between them, and with the smoothness of inevitability enclosed her unresisting body within the loose circle of his arms.

'Look at me, Petra,' he pleaded huskily, 'tell me that you can forgive the wounds inflicted by a man staring into the sweet innocent face of defeat! A man whose isolated citadel was stormed by a loving assailant dressed in the simple white habit of purity. I adore you, *kallista!*' he stressed desperately. 'Whenever I am with you or without you, I see only you!'

His tortured cry struck deep, tapping the source of a fathomless well of emotion that surged and overflowed, sweeping her weakened body into his waiting net.

'Stelios, my darling, I love you so much!' she sobbed, raising sweet lips towards his tormented mouth, to be consumed by his fire, lifted by his flame, melted into a vortex of hot Greek sun, burning kisses, fiery endearments, and the molten passion of a virile, hot-blooded male ...

The noonday sun was long past its peak when she stirred, reluctant to abandon the almost sinful contentment of his embrace. They were lying stretched out beneath the trees in the orange orchard, protected from the heat by a canopy of branches, when she drew herself upright and twisted round to lean over Stelio's sleeping form. Her heart ached with love as she searched for signs of the boy who had been reared to hide every trace of heartache; the man who had withdrawn into an unemotional shell designed to protect him from unwanted intimacy; the lover who had swept away all doubts by subjugating pride in order to bare his soul and discovered the innocence of youth in lowered lashes; a lingering shadow of suffering on strained features; a vulnerable tenderness softening lips that had recently been drained of passion.

'Stelios,' she nudged him awake, reluctant to allow even sleep to come between them.

'What is it, *kallista,* my beautiful, adorable, deep-breasted goddess?' he teased, too lazily content to lift dense black lashes.

Her bones seemed to melt with tenderness when his hands sought for her waist to draw her down towards him. But she resisted their pressure, determined not to court seduction until he had rid her of doubt.

'Why *me*, Stelios? Why, of all the beautiful

women you have known, did you choose to fall in love with me?'

Dark lashes winged upward, revealing slumbrous eyes showing a stirring of hunger in their depths that made her feel wanton—and at the same time shy.

'Unlike Heracles, I was given no choice.' He pretended to scowl, obviously disinclined to be serious.

'What has Heracles to do with us?' she scolded, unknowingly cancelling out the sting of acerbity in her tone with an enchanting dimple.

He sighed, resigning himself to having to waste precious time talking.

'When Heracles was a youth he was accosted by Virtue and Pleasure and asked to choose between them. Pleasure promised him all physical delights, but Virtue promised immortality. He chose Virtue—whereas *I* had virtue thrust upon me!' He pounced, pulling her into his arms with the desperation of a sinner whose appetite for penance has been exhausted. 'I don't wish to hold an inquest into the past, *kallista,* not now that I have the earth, the sun and the moon in my arms—and especially the moon, that symbol of cool femininity, love, peace and mysterious allure,' he groaned, branding a hot kiss of desire upon a cool pale curve of shoulder.

Petra quivered, feeling herself being drawn once more into a sea of ecstasy. But she lingered in the shallows to whisper a last protest.

'But I am so ordinary, Stelios, so . . . so green and immature!'

Sensing her need of reassurance, he leashed his

passion just long enough to pluck with his eyes the blush-pink roses from her cheeks; ivory magnolia buds from her breasts; indigo pansies from eyes soft as velvet, and to bend her body, supple as a willow stem, across his imprisoning arm.

'Those are exactly the qualities I find so enchanting, my prim and pure Miss Grundy! Like fruit plucked from a tree when it is green and tart, you nurtured a secret, impregnable core—then ripened before my eyes into sweet, delectable maturity!'

Harlequin Plus

A WORD ABOUT THE AUTHOR

A small terrace house in northern England, over-shadowed by the towering brick wall of a mill, with the frantic humming of looms forever in the background.... This is the home of Margaret Rome, in which she spins love stories set in France, or in Italy, or on the banks of the Amazon.

Her first job was at a bakery, where her father, mother, sister and two brothers worked. She left there to be married and, after the birth of a son, took part-time work as an usherette, printer, waitress and shop assistant. Then came college, a teacher who inspired his writing class to reach new heights, and an announcement to her family one holiday weekend: "I think I'll write a book."

As good as her word, she completed her first manuscript in twelve weeks. Today, many romance novels later, Margaret Rome confesses that "it's still a thrill to see my name in print."

Take these **4** best-selling novels **FREE**

Your FREE gift includes

Anne Mather—Born out of Love
Violet Winspear—Time of the Temptress
Charlotte Lamb—Man's World
Sally Wentworth—Say Hello to Yesterday

FREE Gift Certificate
and subscription reservation

Mail this coupon today!

Harlequin Reader Service

In the U.S.A.
1440 South Priest Drive
Tempe, AZ 85281

In Canada
649 Ontario Street
Stratford, Ontario N5A 6W2

Please send me my 4 Harlequin Presents books free. Also, reserve a subscription to the 8 new Harlequin Presents novels published each month. Each month I will receive 8 new Presents novels at the low price of $1.75 each [Total— $14.00 a month]. There are no shipping and handling or any other hidden charges. I am free to cancel at any time, but even if I do, these first 4 books are still mine to keep absolutely FREE without any obligation. 108 BPP CADC

NAME _____ (PLEASE PRINT)

ADDRESS _____ APT. NO. _____

CITY _____

STATE/PROV. _____ ZIP/POSTAL CODE _____

Offer expires September 28, 1984

If price changes are necessary you will be notified.